OUT OF CONTROL

"You seem to think that everyone owes you an apology these days, Aaron," Jeffrey responded hotly. "But maybe you're the one who should be doing it, like apologizing to Brad, for one!"

"Oh, yeah? So now you're against me, too, right?"

"Jeez, Aaron! Grow up, will you? Stop acting like a spoiled brat."

Suddenly Aaron lost whatever control he had left, and before anyone realized what was happening, he threw himself at Jeffrey and punched him in the mouth.

"Jeffrey!" Elizabeth screamed.

The impact threw him backward into the crowd, and there was a moment of shocked silence. All eyes were on Aaron Dallas as he looked down at his best friend, an expression of utter disbelief and horror on his face.

Bantam Books in the Sweet Valley High Series
Ask your bookseller for the books you have missed

SWEET VALLEY HIGH

OUT OF CONTROL

Written by
Kate William

Created by
FRANCINE PASCAL

BANTAM BOOKS
TORONTO • NEW YORK • LONDON • SYDNEY • AUCKLAND

RL6, IL age 12 and up

OUT OF CONTROL
A Bantam Book / March 1987

Sweet Valley High is a trademark of Francine Pascal.

Conceived by Francine Pascal

Produced by Cloverdale Press, Inc.

Cover art by James Mathewuse

ISBN 0-553-26341-2

Published simultaneously in the United States and Canada

Bantam Books are published by Bantam Books, Inc. Its trademark, consisting of
the words "Bantam Books" and the portrayal of a rooster, is Registered in
U.S. Patent and Trademark Office and in other countries. Marca Registrada.
Bantam Books, Inc., 666 Fifth Avenue, New York, New York 10103.

PRINTED IN THE UNITED STATES OF AMERICA

O   0 9 8 7 6 5 4 3 2 1

To Casey Bernstein

One

Elizabeth Wakefield gave her golden-blond hair a final stroke with the brush and checked her watch: four o'clock, just enough time to get to school and catch the last few minutes of Jeffrey's soccer practice.

The thought of spending even a little time watching her boyfriend brought a smile to her lips. She winked at her reflection in the bathroom mirror and turned to walk back into her bedroom. But when she heard a sound behind the other connecting door, she changed her mind.

"Hi, Jess! When did you get home?" she called, her hand on the knob.

She paused for a moment, expecting an answer. But there was only silence from the other room. "I must be hearing things," she told herself. But she decided to check anyway and opened the door to her identical twin's room.

1

Most people would be more than a little taken aback by Jessica Wakefield's room. One day, on a whim, Jessica had painted the walls dark brown. And to add to the dark, cavelike feeling, every surface was covered with clothes, magazines, Sweet Dreams romances, and more clothes. But Elizabeth was accustomed to "The Hershey Bar," as the room was known in her family, and she barely noticed it as she looked for her sister.

Jessica was lying on her stomach on the floor beside the bed, propped up on her elbows. Her blond hair was falling forward into her face, and her long, denim-clad legs were stretched out behind her. She absentmindedly fingered the gold lavaliere that hung from her neck. It was identical to the one Elizabeth wore, and both were presents for their sixteenth birthday.

Identical down to the dimples in their left cheeks, the two were separated in age by only four minutes. Elizabeth was the "big sister," and Jessica loved to tease her about it. But right then Jessica was absorbed in reading a multicolored brochure. She seemed oblivious to Elizabeth.

The tail of a handsome golden Labrador puppy thumped softly on a pile of clothes in a corner.

"Hi, Prince Albert!" Elizabeth called to the puppy.

Prince Albert scrambled to his feet and ran over to greet her.

"Who's the zombie over there?" she asked, picking him up.

He licked her cheek, ecstactic to see her. Elizabeth sat down on the bed and scratched the puppy's ears. Still Jessica did not look up.

"Jess, just what is so fascinating that you can't even say hello to your own sister?" She leaned over so she could read the artistically styled lettering on the leaflet: " 'Tofu-Glo'? What on earth is that?" Elizabeth asked.

Heaving a sigh, Jessica finally tore her eyes away from her reading and looked up at her sister. "Tofu-Glo just happens to be a product that's going to make me a millionaire." With that startling announcement, she turned back to the brochure.

Elizabeth let out a peal of astonished laughter. "Oh, really, Jess? And how is it going to do that?"

"Don't laugh," Jessica said, the expression in her blue-green eyes serious as she pushed herself up from the floor. "It's really great. Tons of Tofu-Glo girls make thousands of dollars selling the stuff." She tossed the brochure into Elizabeth's lap then sat down on her bed, pulling Prince Albert toward her.

3

"Tofu-Glo is a line of beauty and health products made from soybeans," she continued as she tickled Prince Albert's stomach. "It's totally natural, and people go crazy for it. I bet I can sell a hundred and thirty-seven tons of the stuff."

Elizabeth shook her head in amazement as she hastily scanned the Tofu-Glo literature. It sounded a little fishy to her. Cosmetics made from soybeans? "Are you really serious?" she asked.

Jessica nodded emphatically, her blue-green eyes wide with excitement. "Just read the whole thing, Liz, OK? There's shampoo and facial cleanser, moisturizer, and some kind of diet supplement."

"Hmm. 'Tofu-Shampu,' 'Soya-Soft.' Jess, this stuff sounds disgusting!"

"Just read it, please?"

After a skeptical glance at her twin, Elizabeth turned her full attention to the Tofu-Glo brochure. There were testimonials from Tofu-Glo girls on how much money they made, and there were endorsements from satisfied customers. One woman claimed that Soya-Soft moisturizer had made all her wrinkles disappear, and a Tofu-Glo girl from San Diego said she was putting her son through college on her sales of Tofu-Shampu alone.

The brochure made it sound as though

selling the products and making lots of money were easy. But Elizabeth, a reporter for *The Oracle*, the school newspaper at Sweet Valley High, knew enough to be suspicious of anything that sounded so simple. Her reporter's instinct was on "red alert" instantly.

On the other hand, if there was one person who would make a good salesperson, it had to be Jessica Wakefield. She could be funny, persuasive, and enthusiastic about anything she wanted anyone to do for her; Elizabeth knew that very well. More than once she had told herself not to agree to some plan of her twin's, but miraculously she would find herself up to her neck in it anyway. And, Elizabeth thought, if Jessica did try to sell health and beauty products, she had to be successful because she was so healthy and beautiful, a walking advertisement.

Elizabeth cast a sidelong glance at her twin. They did look identical, but on the inside, they were as different as could be. Elizabeth liked to take things slowly, liked to follow conventional paths. But Jessica! Jessica was always jumping from one thing to another, her enthusiasm running in high gear all the time.

Right then Jessica was looking at her hopefully, and Elizabeth realized that her opinion meant a lot to her twin. She drew a deep breath.

"I know you'll be great," she said, giving her sister a big hug. "I'll even buy some of it myself."

"I knew you'd see it my way," Jesscia said, jumping up in a rush. "For starters I'll have a Tofu-Glo party, you know, invite everybody over and tell them all about it. It'll be so much fun!" She paced back and forth in a burst of frenetic exuberance. "I thought I could invite all the girls from Pi Beta Alpha over a week from Wednesday. I'll have the party then."

Elizabeth found herself getting caught up in Jessica's enthusiasm. She didn't even care that it would mean actually attending a sorority meeting. She usually avoided them. All that the PBA sorority did, in her opinion, was get together to gossip. She had joined because Jessica asked her to, but she had very little to do with it. "Good idea," she said. "But why wait until then? Can't you start sooner?"

"I need to get my sales pitch ready. I don't want to start selling until I've got it perfect. Besides, by then I'll have my samples."

That was a practical idea for Jessica, Elizabeth thought. It sounded as though her sister was giving her new project quite a lot of thought.

"And I'll invite some girls who aren't in PBA, too. I want to have everybody I know come."

Prince Albert, caught up in their excitement, looked eagerly from one girl to the other. He let out an enthusiastic yip. The twins laughed, and as Jessica sat down again on the bed, they continued planning.

"Will you go door-to-door, too?" Elizabeth asked. "You'll have to rehearse your sales pitch, so you sound professional."

"Oh, right. You can help me with that, Liz." Jessica looked eagerly into her sister's face and bit her lower lip. "I really want to be good."

"You will be, Jess. I know you will."

"There's only one problem," she said, nervously pleating the material of her bedspread. She looked up quickly. "I need a hundred and fifty dollars to buy the starter kit, and I've only got a hundred. So can I borrow fifty dollars?" she finished in a rush, her face a picture of anxious anticipation.

Elizabeth's heart sank. She knew that when Jessica borrowed money she meant to pay it back, but somehow she almost never did. It wasn't that Elizabeth wasn't glad to help her twin, but it took a lot of baby-sitting to make fifty dollars.

Obviously, Jessica knew her well enough to sense the hesitation Elizabeth felt. "OK, forget it. It doesn't matter," she cried, turning away melodramatically. "I'll have to ask Lila, I guess."

"Jessica, you know perfectly well you'd never borrow money from Lila Fowler." Jessica's friend was one of the richest girls in Sweet Valley, and she never let Jessica forget it.

Jessica pouted. "Well it's not as if she couldn't afford to lend me fifty dollars."

"But, Jess, why do you have to start out by handing over a hundred and fifty dollars? It doesn't make much sense to me."

"But I'll make it all back selling just a third of the stuff I get. Really!" Jessica grabbed her sister's hand. "Please, Lizzie? I'll pay you right back, I swear!"

"OK, OK! I give up!" Elizabeth laughed. "I can't have you begging in the streets, can I?" she teased.

"Oh, I knew you would!" Jessica was instantly happy again. "That means I can get started right away. I'll call them right now and tell them I'm signing up." She began tossing her clothes around, searching for her telephone. "Hey, look! Here's that scarf I thought I lost," she announced.

Elizabeth laughed and stood up, suddenly realizing how late she would be meeting Jeffrey. "OK, young Miss Entrepreneur, I'll give you the money tomorrow. See you later."

She left her sister trying to find the phone by tracing the cord from the wall. She then ran down the stairs and out the door. Within minutes she was driving the red Fiat convertible that she and Jessica shared down the tree-lined streets of Sweet Valley, and she smiled to herself as she looked around. Elizabeth loved their quiet California town. It was big enough to be interesting and exciting, yet small enough so that everyone felt like a neighbor. She told herself for the thousandth time that she would never want to live anywhere else.

Soon she turned into the Sweet Valley High driveway and deftly pulled the Fiat into a parking spot.

As she made her way across campus to the playing fields, she thought again about Jessica's new scheme. Her sister was always getting involved in one money-making scheme after another. Like the time in the sixth grade, when she was supposed to take care of a neighbor's dog for a few days. But she managed to sneak off to a concert, and the dog ran away unnoticed. That was a nightmare! Maybe this time things would be different. Tofu products might be strange, but then, Elizabeth reminded herself, people would buy almost anything.

Coach Horner's whistle blew shrilly as Elizabeth climbed up into the bleachers, her steps making a dull *thunk-clunk* on the wooden treads. Her eyes darted over the field, following the players as they raced back and forth with the soccer ball.

Finally she saw the tall, athletic figure of Jeffrey French, and her heart gave a delighted little thump. They had been going out for a few months, since shortly after Jeffrey moved to Sweet Valley from Oregon.

She had never dreamed they'd fall in love. But she and Jeffrey had been irresistibly drawn to each other, and now she couldn't imagine not loving him.

As if he felt her looking at him, Jeffrey glanced up from the field and caught her eye. He gave her a friendly salute, then turned just in time to block a pass with his outstretched foot. Elizabeth laughed admiringly and then whistled through her fingers. Jeffrey looked up again and grinned.

"Hey, I thought I might find you here," a familiar voice called up to her from below.

Elizabeth's face lit up. "Enid! Come on up. I've got a great view."

"Yeah, and I can guess what the view is of." Elizabeth's best friend laughed as she climbed up the bleachers.

Enid Rollins sat down and dropped her book bag on the step in front of them. She brushed her brown hair away from her forehead and surveyed the playing field with her green eyes. "He really looks great, Liz. I don't know how you always manage to get the cutest guy around, but you do."

"Oh, you poor thing," Elizabeth said, teasing her. "Remember, you had your chance." When Jeffrey had first moved to town, Elizabeth concocted a scheme to fix Enid up with him. The plan had backfired, but Enid hadn't minded at all. It was still a good joke between them, though.

For a few moments the two girls sat in companionable silence, watching the boys below them. They exchanged a few comments as the scrimmage continued, first on one side then the other. The team was good this year, thanks to Aaron Dallas, the co-captain of the squad. He was a natural at soccer. Whenever his side scored, he was generally the point maker.

Although she usually only watched Jeffrey, Elizabeth found herself observing Aaron more

11

and more. "If we win the finals this year, it'll be because of Aaron," she commented, watching him block a pass with his knee and bounce the ball expertly onto his instep.

As Aaron carefully herded the ball down the field, watching for an opening, Tony Esteban slipped in ahead of him and stole the ball. There was a brief scramble, and the ball went out of bounds.

"It's out on Dallas!" called Tony.

Aaron whirled around to face him. "Are you blind? It went out on you!"

Tony shrugged and shook his head. "No way, Dallas." He turned and walked away.

With an angry cry Aaron raced after Tony and pulled him around. "What do you think you're doing, calling a foul on me?"

The rest of the players crowded around, and Elizabeth and Enid leaned forward, trying to make out what was going on. All they could hear was Aaron Dallas, yelling and swearing at Tony.

"What's going on down there?" asked Enid. "Did Tony do something to Aaron?"

Elizabeth shook her head impatiently. "I think they just collided. I'm not really sure."

But apparently Aaron was not going to take the call, and he kept yelling at Tony, demanding that he agree. Coach Horner was running toward the knot of soccer players as

Jeffrey French stepped forward and took Aaron's arm. Elizabeth couldn't hear Jeffrey's words, but he was obviously trying to calm Aaron down.

The two boys moved away from the other players. Aaron was gesturing angrily and pointing back at Tony as Jeffrey led him away.

"OK!" yelled Coach Horner, stepping into the group. "Time to pack it in! Hit the showers!"

By ones and twos the soccer players drifted away from the crowd and headed for the gym and locker room. The coach stalked over to Aaron and Jeffrey, and the three had a short, obviously tense conference. Then the two boys started for the locker room.

"I can't believe it!" Elizabeth said finally, shaking her head impatiently. "Aaron has been acting weird lately! Remember the way he got so upset when someone stepped on his foot at Lila's party?"

Enid nodded slowly. "I know. I don't know what it is, but he's been angry at everybody. The other day I saw him arguing with Robin Wilson. He said she cheated off him on a math test, and she told me later she had just leaned down to pick up her pencil! Something must really be bothering him."

With a momentary pang of sympathy, Elizabeth remembered that there was something:

She knew Aaron was having some sort of family problems. Jeffrey had told her that a few days before, and he said that it might be serious. But whatever it was, Aaron had been getting more and more short-tempered. Now it seemed that almost anything could infuriate him.

And it was hurting him, too. He used to be popular and friendly, but now he was only angry, impatient, and defensive. A lot of people were getting tired of his irrationality and hypersensitivity. Aaron was slowly losing all his friends.

Except for Jeffrey French. He and Aaron had met at a soccer camp the previous summer, before Jeffrey moved to Sweet Valley. There was a special bond between them.

Now it seemed that Jeffrey was the only one willing to put up with Aaron, the only one willing to give him a chance. And that was worrying Elizabeth more and more. She sympathized with Aaron over his family problems, but she could not forgive him for letting his emotions run so wild. It was irritating to see him not even try to control his temper.

It would be one thing if it had hurt only him. But almost everyone at Sweet Valley High had been affected by his temper recently. And he seemed to expect sympathy, no matter what he had done. Elizabeth Wakefield used to like Aaron a lot. But her sympathy was running out now. She watched her boyfriend and Aaron as they disappeared through the locker room door.

"You don't know how lucky you are," she muttered.

"Huh?"

Elizabeth turned to Enid and gave her an apologetic smile. "Sorry, I'm just being grumpy." She nodded in the direction of the gym. "Jeffrey spends a lot of time with Aaron, that's all. And half the time now, I don't think Aaron deserves a friend like him."

Two

"Stop pacing, Liz. You're making me dizzy."

Elizabeth shot Enid a guilty smile and tried to calm down. For some reason, Aaron's near-fight on the soccer field had left her worried and agitated. They were outside the boys' locker room, waiting for Jeffrey to come out.

"Sorry," she muttered through clenched teeth.

Enid pushed herself away from the wall and glanced at the clock above the locker room door. "Listen, Jeffrey will be out in a minute. I'm going to go, OK? I'll talk to you later."

"Sure. Bye." Elizabeth watched her friend until she disappeared around a corner. Then unconsciously she began pacing again as she waited for Jeffrey.

At that moment the door opened behind her, and she whirled around, ready to speak.

But it wasn't Jeffrey. Restraining an impatient sigh, Elizabeth leaned against the wall.

She realized then that she was more than a little upset about Aaron Dallas and about Jeffrey's unswerving loyalty to him. For a moment she tried to convince herself that she was being selfish or unreasonable about Aaron. But when she remembered how easily he had exploded during a routine soccer practice, she began worrying again. She was afraid that not even Jeffrey would get by without having Aaron turn on him. And she knew that would be a painful blow to him. It was too much to hope that Aaron would never lash out at Jeffrey.

"Well, you look like the happiest person in the world right now," a voice murmured in her ear.

"Oh!" She spun around and received a quick kiss on the mouth. "Hi!" she said breathlessly, smiling in spite of her gloomy thoughts.

"Hi, yourself!" Jeffrey's face was glowing, and his blond hair was slicked back, wet from his shower. Elizabeth felt a warm rush of happiness as she looked up and met his steady gaze.

After a moment Jeffrey broke eye contact with a quick grin. "Hold my books a minute, OK?" he asked, handing them to Elizabeth.

As he shrugged into his varsity jacket, she

drew a deep breath. "So, what was that business with Aaron all about?" she began, wishing she didn't feel that she had to bring it up.

"Tony made a bad call, that's all," Jeffrey replied, taking his books from her. "Thanks."

"Sure. Well, why did Aaron get so mad?"

Jeffrey met her serious gaze with a puzzled look of his own. "He had a pretty good reason to get mad. He thought it was a lousy call."

"But that mad? Aaron always seems to have a good excuse for getting angry," Elizabeth persisted. "He seems to get mad at everything and anything these days."

"Well," Jeffrey said, "maybe I shouldn't tell you this, but his parents are getting divorced. His mom left Mr. Dallas for another man."

"Oh, that's awful!" said Elizabeth.

"Yeah, and Aaron's having a tough time getting used to it. He's living with his dad, and I get the feeling that he's pretty strict." He smiled softly as he took Elizabeth's hand. "Just try to be fair about it, OK? Try to understand."

"But I have tried." She paused a moment. Had she really tried? she wondered. "It's just that I don't think he's really trying to control himself."

"Control himself? Come on, Liz. You make him sound like a psychopath."

"Oh, Jeffrey, listen to me! I don't know why you keep defending him. I'm really sorry his parents are getting divorced and everything, but he shouldn't inflict his problems on the whole school. He's been lashing out at everybody." She turned away as the locker room door opened and a group of boys came out.

"Hey, see you later, Jeff."

Jeffrey waved to his teammates. "See you later."

The two watched silently as the boys walked down the hall, and the scene on the soccer field flashed vividly before Elizabeth's eyes again.

"What do the other guys think about the way he's acting?" she asked, nodding her head in their direction.

"I guess they're not too crazy about it. And the coach has really come down hard on him for it." He shook his head as if remembering something he had tried to forget. "He even told Aaron once a couple of weeks ago he'd be benched if he didn't get it together."

"And did he?"

Jeffrey shrugged again. "For a few days, I guess. Look, Liz," Jeffrey went on, "I think you should really try to give the guy a break."

Suddenly Elizabeth felt tired. "Maybe you're right, Jeffrey. Let's just forget about it, OK?"

He put his arm around her shoulders and pulled her to him. "Sure. Let's not fight about it."

Elizabeth nodded. Their relationship had never been totally argument-free, but somehow this disagreement was making her feel worse than some of the others they'd had.

"Hey, Jeffrey, you're still here."

Elizabeth and Jeffrey moved apart quickly and turned to the door. Aaron was slipping into his jacket, the old friendly smile on his handsome face.

That's the Aaron I used to know, Elizabeth realized sadly.

"So are we still on for tonight?" Aaron continued, still smiling at them.

Elizabeth looked quickly at Jeffrey, a question in her blue-green eyes.

"I told Aaron we're going to a movie tonight, so he and Heather are going to meet us there," he explained, avoiding her gaze.

There wasn't much Elizabeth could say with Aaron standing right there. But the thought of a double date with Aaron and his new girlfriend, Heather Sanford, did not fill her with enthusiasm just then. She really wanted to be alone with Jeffrey that night.

And besides, Elizabeth was fast losing patience with Aaron. And she didn't really know his new girlfriend, a sophomore. From the little she knew about her, the girl seemed empty headed. All Heather talked about were clothes and Aaron.

But Elizabeth could hardly tell Jeffrey she wanted to be alone with him while Aaron was still there, so she managed a smile. "OK, see you later, Aaron."

As Elizabeth and Jeffrey drove back through Sweet Valley to the Wakefield house, an uneasy silence lay between them. After their earlier discussion, Elizabeth didn't want to bring up the subject again. But she was disappointed that she would have to spend her Friday night with two people she didn't like very much.

She pulled the car into the driveway, and the two walked up the path to the comfortable split-level ranch house.

"Liz? Is that you?" Mrs. Wakefield's voice called from the kitchen as Elizabeth and Jeffrey walked through the front door.

"Yes, Mom."

Alice Wakefield came into the living room, wiping her hands on a dish towel. "Hi, sweetie. Hi, Jeffrey." Blond and tanned, Mrs. Wakefield was still slim enough to fit into her daughters' size six clothing. She looked more like the twins' older sister than their mother.

"We're having a Mexican feast tonight," she said with a smile. "So come help with the chopping and grating. I don't know why Mexican food has to be in little pieces, but that's the way it is.

"How was soccer today, Jeffrey?" Mrs. Wakefield continued, leading them back into the kitchen.

"Pretty good," he replied, smiling at Elizabeth. "We're definitely going to the play-offs this year against Big Mesa."

"I think that's wonderful. Now if you could just take this cheese, Jeffrey, and zap it through the food processor, that'd be great. Hand me that knife, would you, Liz?"

Elizabeth passed her mother the knife and leaned against the sink, watching her. Alice Wakefield never seemed to run out of energy. She worked all day at her successful interior design business and then came home to run the Wakefield household as smoothly as any full-time housewife.

"You're pretty special, Mom," she whispered, giving her mother a quick hug.

Mrs. Wakefield turned with a delighted smile on her face. "Well, what did I do to deserve that?" She laughed.

Elizabeth grinned. "Oh, I don't know."

"Deserve what?" Ned Wakefield, the twins' father, asked as he entered the kitchen. He put his briefcase down on the kitchen table and kissed his wife. "Hi, Liz. How are you, Jeffrey?"

"Fine, Mr. Wakefield, thanks," Jeffrey replied, shaking the lawyer's hand.

"Jeffrey says Sweet Valley is going to the soccer finals this year," Mrs. Wakefield said, smiling at her husband.

"Oh, yeah? That's great, Jeff. I bet it's partly because of Aaron Dallas, right? He was really good last weekend."

Jeffrey nodded enthusiastically. "Absolutely. We'd never have made it this far without him."

"A fur coat!" Jessica announced suddenly, making a typically dramatic entrance into the bright, Spanish-tiled kitchen. She spotted her sister's boyfriend and threw him a brilliant smile. "Hi, Jeff. Hi, Daddy."

Mrs. Wakefield laughed. "A fur coat what, Jess?"

With a toss of her blond head, Jessica sat down and started munching on a handful of tortilla chips. "That's what I'm going to buy first," she mumbled. She swallowed. "Mink."

Her parents exchanged a surprised glance. "That sounds a bit warm for Southern California, Jessica," Ned Wakefield observed. "But just for the record, how are you planning to buy this mink coat?"

Elizabeth shook her head and smiled. She signaled to Jeffrey to help her set the table as her twin explained her new enterprise.

"Doesn't it sound absolutely fantastic? I mean, I can't lose," Jessica concluded with a confident smile. "Everyone will want to buy Tofu-Glo from me, and I'll make a fortune."

"Sounds pretty gross to me," Jeffrey whispered in Elizabeth's ear.

She restrained a giggle and handed him a stack of Mexican earthenware plates.

"Just how thoroughly have you researched this company, Jessica?" Mr. Wakefield asked casually. He poured himself a drink and took a sip, looking at his ambitious daughter over the rim of his glass. "There are a lot of dishonest firms out there."

"Oh, Dad! Do you think I'd get involved in something that wasn't completely legit?"

He smiled wryly. "I think I'll pass on that one. I'm kidding, honey," he added hastily as Jessica's face took on a look of comic indignation. "All I'm saying is that you might find yourself caught up in something with unpleasant surprises. That's all."

"Dad, you don't—"

"Oh, I don't know, dear," Alice cut in, turning from the stove. She smiled warmly at Jessica. "I sold cleaning products once—door-to-door—while I was in college, remember?

And to tell you the truth, I thought it was a lot of fun." She gave the saucepan of cheese dip a quick stir and shrugged. "I think it would be a good experience."

"There, see!" crowed Jessica triumphantly. "Mom thinks it's a good idea."

"Yeah, Dad," Elizabeth added. "Steven sold magazine subscriptions when he was in the Boy Scouts, remember?" Steven Wakefield, the twins' older brother, a freshman in a nearby college, lived in a dorm, but he often came home for weekends. "You didn't mind him doing it."

"OK, OK!" Her father laughed. "But you won't object if I make a few 'discreet inquiries' into this Tofu-Glo company, now, will you? Or would you consider that an invasion of your privacy?"

Jessica shrugged. "I don't care."

"Good. But, Jess, how are you going to find time for this? On top of cheerleading, the sorority, and taking care of Prince Albert?"

"Dad, don't worry!"

He shrugged. "All right, all right! If you're sure?"

"I'm sure."

"OK. Now how about dinner?"

Jessica was so full of enthusiasm for Tofu-Glo that she could hardly sit still while they ate. She kept talking about what she would do when she was "disgustingly rich." By the end of the meal, Elizabeth's gloomy mood had vanished.

But when she and Jeffrey were getting ready to leave, she felt a twinge of disappointment return. She was not looking forward to this double date at all. She had a nagging suspicion that by the end of the night she'd regret having agreed to go.

Three

"Pour us some more champagne, Teddie."

"But, Lady Ashley, do you really think it's wise? It's a dangerous night—"

"Oh, Teddie! That's precisely what I mean! Don't say no to me tonight. All of Paris awaits us!"

Elizabeth sighed as she reached for some more popcorn, enthralled by the turn-of-the-century romance unfolding on the screen. With Jeffrey's arm warm across her shoulders, she finally began to enjoy the evening. She settled back, snuggling into Jeffrey's side. There was no place she'd rather be than right there.

"Don't you love movies like this?" Heather Sanford whispered from Elizabeth's left.

With a short, silent nod, Elizabeth agreed, and stared straight ahead.

"The way you look just now, the moonlight shining on your lovely face—your eyes, your lips. I—"

"I think it's incredibly romantic," came Heather's whispering voice again as she leaned closer. "Especially her. She's so glamorous."

Restraining an impatient sigh, Elizabeth nodded again. She knew Heather was just trying to be friendly, but the girl's timing was awful, Elizabeth thought.

She stole a glance at Jeffrey's profile in the darkened theater, wondering if he was enjoying the movie as much as she was. They usually agreed on what they liked. That was one of the things she loved about being with him. No matter what they were doing, they always had a good time together. She turned back to the screen.

The leading lady sat at a grand piano, her fingers moving idly over the keys. Teddie stared forlornly at her from a tasseled sofa. Their eyes met, and the music swelled.

"Give me a cigarette," Lady Ashley whispered, turning quickly away. Her eyes were bright with unshed tears.

"Look at that dress! That lace is just unbelievable!"

"Heather, please!" Elizabeth urged hoarsely. "Why don't we talk about it later, OK?"

"Oh, sure, sure. Sorry."

Elizabeth closed her eyes briefly, telling herself to be patient. But it seemed as if Heather had gotten the message. Elizabeth was able to enjoy the rest of the movie uninterrupted.

"Oh," she said later, wiping away a tear as they shuffled up the aisle under the lights, "I always feel so dumb, crying in the movies." She sent Jeffrey a shamefaced smile, and he tightened his arm around her.

"You're just a sentimental slob, that's all, Liz. She cries at everything, even the credits," he added wickedly to Aaron.

"Oh, so do I!" Heather sighed ecstatically. "I completely fall apart watching almost any romantic movie, especially if it's set in the past. Even the music can make me cry! And the costumes are always so incredible!"

Elizabeth turned to Jeffery and rolled her eyes. Couldn't Heather talk about anything but clothes?

Heather was obsessed, Elizabeth had decided after meeting her just once. And she didn't spare any energy when it came to her own wardrobe. For that simple evening at the movies, she had chosen to wear an impeccably tailored olive green dress, the collar and cuffs faced with buttery-soft green suede. Of course, Elizabeth admitted, Heather looked striking in it, as usual. But wasn't it a little elaborate for the Valley Cinema?

"Let's hit Casey's, OK?" suggested Aaron

as they emerged from the theater into the cool evening air. "After that movie I could really use a Casey double deluxe."

The others agreed readily, and soon the four were ensconced in one of the cozy booths at one of Sweet Valley High's favorite hangouts. The old-fashioned ice-cream parlor was packed with local kids. Several people called out greetings as they sat down.

"Two Casey double deluxes, one dish mocha chip," repeated the harried waitress as she glanced at her pad. She turned to Heather. "What about you, hon?"

Heather blushed. "Oh, just a Diet Coke, please. That's all I want."

Elizabeth registered that without batting an eyelash. She already knew Heather was always on a diet, probably so she wouldn't outgrow any of her glamorous outfits. It seemed to be another symptom of Heather's vanity.

"So, who liked the movie?" Elizabeth asked. "You already know I'm a sentimental slob, so it doesn't matter what I thought of it."

Jeffrey surveyed her with a mocking smile. "Goes with being a dumb blond, the sentimental slob part."

She landed a light punch on Jeffrey's shoulder. "Be careful, Buster."

"Well, I thought it was just beautiful,"

Heather answered, a dreamy look on her face. "And you just knew they'd be passionately in love for the rest of their lives. It was so—so real, you know?"

Aaron grimaced sourly. "Oh, come on. Real life is never like that. People fall out of love, believe me."

"Aaron! That's not very nice!" his girlfriend protested with a little pout.

"Well, it's true."

Elizabeth glanced at Jeffrey from the corner of her eye. She knew love could be like the movie. Her parents were obviously still very much in love, even after more than twenty years of marriage.

But then, that was probably why Aaron was so cynical. His parents' love hadn't lasted. There was no "happily ever after" for the Dallases now that they were divorcing.

A throb of sympathetic pain touched Elizabeth's heart. It must be terrible for Aaron, she realized. And she made a vow to try to be more understanding with him in the future.

"Hey, look, there are some of the guys on the team," Jeffrey said, turning to look across the ice-cream parlor. He turned back to the girls. "Mind if we go talk to them for a minute?"

For a moment Elizabeth wished she could

say yes. She didn't want to be left alone with Heather. But she knew she couldn't.

"Go ahead," Heather chirped. "It'll give Liz and me a chance for some girl talk." She waggled her fingers at Aaron. "Bye-bye."

Elizabeth was a little surprised. She never thought of herself as someone who talked "girl talk."

As the two boys slid out from the booth, Heather leaned her elbows on the table. "I'm really glad they left, so we can talk."

With a sinking heart, Elizabeth watched Jeffrey's retreating figure. She was sure that Heather wouldn't have anything very interesting to say. She'd probably just talk about clothes and Aaron, her two favorite topics of conversation.

Heather seemed determined to tell Elizabeth her whole life's story in the next five minutes. To her closest friends, Elizabeth was a great listener, and she was always willing to help out with any advice she could give. But that kind of soul baring from a casual acquaintance made her extremely uncomfortable.

"And when I graduate I want to go to a fashion institute," she heard Heather say.

"Oh, really? That's great," Elizabeth mumbled, her eyes on the table of soccer players across the room. A voice was raised, and even through the noise of the crowd, Elizabeth sensed a sharp increase in the level of intensity.

"What about you?" asked Heather.

"What? Oh, I'm sorry," Elizabeth stammered, focusing on Heather again. She paused, wondering if there was a polite way to discourage her. She wasn't sure the subtle approach would work. "I'm really sort of a private person, Heather," she said, a delicate blush coloring her tanned cheeks.

Heather looked up as the waitress came with their order. "Thanks. I understand, Liz," she said, her voice slightly subdued.

Elizabeth felt a pang of guilt and wondered whether Heather believed her. She dug into her mocha chip ice cream. Across from her, Heather quietly sipped her Coke. After a few moments of awkward silence, Elizabeth began to wonder if she should say something. But she couldn't think of anything Heather might relate to.

"That's a lie!" Aaron's voice cut sharply through the usual Friday night clamor.

The two girls turned quickly in their seats, craning their necks to see what was going on with the soccer players at the other table.

"Hold on, Aaron," Jeffrey began, his voice low but clear.

Aaron, his face clouded with anger, shook off Jeffrey's restraining hand. His chest heaving, he faced Michael Schmidt, the other co-captain, across the crowded table.

"The call was good, Dallas," Michael insisted. "Tony called it right."

"Tony's a liar!" His voice quivering with rage, Aaron leaned across the table, and grabbed Michael's shirt.

Michael's voice rose in pitch as he slapped Aaron's hand away. "Maybe you're the liar, not Tony!"

"Who do you think you're calling a liar, Schmidt?"

Elizabeth looked frantically at Jeffrey, who now took Aaron's arm more forcibly. Almost everyone in Casey's Place was staring at the group of boys.

"Come on, man. Let's drop it, OK? Just forget it."

Still glaring angrily, Aaron allowed Jeffrey to lead him away. When the two boys rejoined Elizabeth and Heather, he was still shaking.

"He's such a liar," he muttered, his clenched fist pressed onto the table.

His knuckles were white as he tightened his fist. Elizabeth tried to catch Jeffrey's eye, but he was too busy trying to smooth over the incident.

"It was hard to see, that's all. A bad angle. Forget about it, Aaron."

At that point Heather reached across the table and started to run her forefinger up and down Aaron's arm. "Is Aaron angry 'bout somethin'?" she cooed, her voice as cuddly cute as a cartoon baby's. "Don' be gwumpy."

"Oh, I'm just mad," Aaron grumbled.

"But Heather doesn't want Aaron to be mad."

Elizabeth felt the beginnings of a blush heat her face as she witnessed this new facet of Heather and Aaron's relationship. It was acutely embarrassing to her to listen to anyone baby-talking unless it was a joke. And this was obviously no joke. Heather was pouting and coaxing Aaron out of his bad mood.

Soon Heather had Aaron completely over his irrational rage. But Elizabeth was shocked. The two of them were like a couple of kindergartners, she thought in amazement. They threw temper tantrums and talked baby talk!

"Jeffrey, I think it's getting kind of late," she said, finally pulling herself together. She met his eye and wordlessly communicated how urgently she wanted to leave.

"You're right," he agreed, obviously a little embarrassed himself. He took out his wallet and placed a couple of bills on the table to cover their share of the check, and he and Elizabeth stood up.

"Bye-bye," Heather said, her eyes still on Aaron.

Aaron looked up, a sheepish grin on his face. "Sorry, Jeffrey. See you later. Bye, Liz."

With a thin smile, Elizabeth nodded, and she and Jeffrey walked quickly out to her car.

"Did Aaron have a good excuse that time?" she asked in a low voice as they pulled out of the parking lot.

Jeffrey's jaw tightened briefly. "Yes," he declared simply.

Four

"Come on, good boy. Bring me the ball."

Prince Albert put his head down on his front paws and wagged his tail. He looked at the yellow tennis ball in front of him. Then he looked at Jessica.

"The ball, Prince Albert. Bring it to me."

When the puppy just looked at her, Jessica rolled her eyes and threw herself on the bed. "You're totally hopeless, you know that? A hundred thirty-seven wild horses couldn't make you fetch."

She stared at the ceiling for a moment, then glanced over at the dog. He was watching her with a deeply mournful expression. It was a face full of reproach. And it was impossible to resist.

"OK! Come on up here, you dope." She laughed and patted the bedspread.

In a burst of ecstasy, Prince Albert grabbed the ball in his mouth and leaped onto Jessica's bed. He dropped the ball on her stomach and rolled over to be tickled.

Jessica giggled. "You're a spoiled little brat, and I'm not—"

The sound of the door bell cut her off. Prince Albert's ears pricked up as she ran to the window to look into the street, where she saw a UPS van parked at the curb. Another impatient chime sent her tearing down the stairs to the front door.

"Hi," she said breathlessly, giving the handsome young delivery man one of her brilliant smiles. "A package for us?"

He glanced at his clipboard and took a pen from behind his ear. "For Jessica Wakefield. She here?"

"That's me. What is it?" She peered eagerly over his shoulder at the van, burning with curiosity.

He grinned. "Sign here, OK?"

After scribbling hastily on the line, Jessica shoved the clipboard back into his hands. "What is it?" she repeated.

"You mean, 'what are *they*?' There's a whole bunch of boxes for you. From the Tofu-Glo Company."

"You're kidding! I can't believe it's already here!" she squealed, dancing with excitement. "Let me help you. Oh, this is great!"

She ran out to the curb and waited impatiently for the UPS man to follow. He sauntered down casually and slid his pen back behind his ear. Then he winked and climbed into the back of his van. Jessica heard him shifting boxes around inside.

"What's taking so long?"

"Here." The first box was thrust into her arms, and she set it down on the sidewalk, ripping off the packing tape with breathless enthusiasm.

"I'll just take these on up to your porch," the man continued, jumping down with several more boxes.

Without answering, Jessica pulled out a plastic bottle labeled "Tofu Shampu."

"Oh, wow," she said, examining the green and gold label.

The delivery man came back and pulled another stack of cartons out of the van.

Jessica pulled out all of the other bottles until she had twelve containers of soy-based shampoo on the sidewalk. She looked at them happily.

"This is going to be so fantastic," she said aloud. She rocked back on her heels, wondering how long it would be before she turned a profit.

The delivery man pulled yet another tower of boxes from the back of the van and carried them unsteadily up the walk to the Wakefields' front door. Finally Jessica looked up from her row of colorful shampoo bottles and blinked in surprise at the stacks on the porch.

"All of that?" she asked, bewildered.

"Not quite," the man replied with a little grunt as he heaved three more boxes onto the sidewalk. "There. That's it. Biggest single delivery this week," he added.

"I—I didn't know there would be so much."

He shrugged. "Don't worry. I hear the stuff is really hot."

Jessica brightened. "Yeah, I know." She looked at the boxes again with growing confidence. After all, she figured, she did pay the Tofu-Glo company a hundred and fifty dollars, so there should be a lot.

Then she grinned. "Hey, don't be surprised if you have another load to deliver pretty soon. I'm going to sell this stuff in no time."

"Well, good luck." The UPS man started the van and pulled away with a goodbye salute.

Jessica repacked the carton of shampoo and carried it up to the porch. Then she proceeded to carry three or four boxes at a time up to her room, where she stacked them in a hastily cleared corner.

By the fourth trip, Jessica's arms were aching, and her new jeans were smudged from wiping her dusty hands on them.

But there were still boxes and boxes of Tofu-Shampu, Tofu-Clean, Soya-Soft, and Soya-Life Dietary Supplement sitting out on the front step. And they were all waiting to be carried up to her room.

"Figures it would come on a day when Liz stays after school," Jessica muttered, wiping her forehead with the back of one grimy hand.

She blew a strand of hair out of her eyes and lifted another box. Prince Albert had already followed her dutifully up and down the stairs several times. But seeing that she wasn't actually going anywhere, he had decided to stand and watch and keep a close eye on her. The chubby, yellow-gold puppy was now surveying her protectively from the top of the stairs.

"Some help you are," Jessica scolded him as she staggered past.

"Well, that's it," she announced breathlessly as she put down the last carton. "You can come in now."

"I can?"

Jessica whirled around. "Liz! You have the worst timing in the world." She made a sour face and folded her arms across her chest.

Her twin laughed. "I try. I try." She approached the towering stack of Tofu-Glo cases. "So, this is your ticket to fiscal happiness, huh?"

43

Jessica threw herself onto the bed and stared bleakly at the cartons. "If I don't die of exhaustion first. But you know," she continued, her spirits lifting again, "I think this could really be it this time, Liz. Know what I mean?" She swung her legs around and rolled off the bed. Grabbing the nearest box, she pulled out a jar of Soya-Soft moisturizing cream.

" 'Soya-Soft cream is a revolution in skin care,' " she read, her voice assuming a dignified, professional tone. " 'Its totally natural ingredients work in harmony to hydrate, tone, and rejuvenate the skin.' "

"Will it make me look years younger?" Elizabeth asked.

Jessica turned the jar over. "Are you kidding? You'll be fifteen again! Let me just read you what's inside." She cleared her throat. " 'Active ingredients: Deionized mineral spring water, soy, aloe vera.' Sounds good so far."

"Oh, tell me more, Tofu-Glo girl!"

Jessica giggled and continued reading. " 'PABA, keratin, peach-kernel oil, essence of beeswax, petroleum, okra extract, fish-bone meal, sebum, hydrolized albumen.' "

By the time she had gotten to the end of the list, Jessica was feeling a little skeptical. But she didn't want Elizabeth to know. "See? It's all totally natural and wonderful."

Elizabeth's mouth was open. She shut it suddenly and swallowed. "Jess, that sounds kind of—"

"Oh, don't be so squeamish," Jessica protested loftily. "It's good for you."

Elizabeth still looked uncertain.

"Well, anyway," Jessica continued breezily, "we've got to start calling people. My Tofu-Glo party is the day after tomorrow, you know."

Her sister shrugged, and they began to compile a list of girls they knew.

"You can even invite Enid if you want," Jessica offered, feeling magnanimous.

Elizabeth raised her eyebrows. "My, how very generous of you."

Jessica could never understand what her twin saw in Enid Rollins. As far as Jessica was concerned, Elizabeth's best friend was incredibly dull. But Elizabeth liked Enid a lot, so she thought she'd show her a little kindness.

Once they were finished, Jessica surveyed the list critically. "It's a pretty big group," she decided. She grinned at Elizabeth. "But the bigger my clientele, the bigger my profits."

"You'll have that mink coat in no time, Jess."

She snorted. "And Lila won't have anything over me anymore." She hadn't told Lila yet about Tofu-Glo. It had been a secret during the research phase. But now that she was officially a Tofu-Glo girl, there was no reason to keep it from Lila any longer, and besides, she was counting on Lila to be one of her best customers. After all, she had plenty of money to spend.

"Listen, I'm going to make some phone calls, OK?"

Elizabeth replaced the jar of Soya-Soft cream in the box. "Sure, I have a story to write anyway."

Jessica wasn't listening. She dragged the phone toward her by the cord and hastily dialed the number of the Fowlers' big hilltop mansion.

"Hi, Lila. It's Jessica, I'm having a party at my house after school on Wednesday," she announced, her voice full of excitement.

"Why?"

"Well . . ." Jessica twirled the phone cord around one finger, trying to give her announcement as much dramatic impact as she could.

"Because I've got a little something to show everyone," she continued mysteriously.

"What is it?"

"Something—special."

"Jessica, would you cut the big buildup and get to the punch line?" Lila sounded like her usual blasé self. But Jessica knew her friend was intrigued.

"OK. I'll tell you. I'm giving a Tofu-Glo party. Isn't that great?"

"Tofu-what?"

"Tofu-Glo is this line of great natural beauty products, and I'm having a party to show it to everyone."

There was silence at the other end of the line. Jessica held her breath.

"Lila?"

"You mean you're selling it?" Lila asked finally.

Jessica grinned. Lila was obviously surprised. "That's right. And I'm going to make a fortune."

There was another pause. When Lila spoke again, her voice was dripping with scorn. "You mean, you're going to be a *salesperson*?"

"Yeah! What's wrong with that?"

"Oh—it's just—well, all I can say is, I'd never do anything so—so déclassé," she finished on a note of smug satisfaction.

Narrowing her eyes, Jessica glared at the phone in her hand. Where did Lila get off being so superior, using words like "déclassé"?

"I'm sure you never would, Lila. I can see how living off your father's money might make it hard for you to take any kind of initiative."

She looked across the room. Elizabeth was watching her from the doorway, a shocked expression on her face. Jessica winked at her and gave her a thumbs-up sign.

There was a third long pause, and Jessica wondered briefly if she'd gone too far. After all, Lila had always had money but not much love. Then again, Lila had no reason to get snotty.

"Well, anyway. Are you coming?"

"Sure," Lila said finally. "I guess so."

Jessica shrugged. She never quite knew what her friend was thinking, but she wasn't going to let that bother her right then. "OK, bye," she said and hung up the phone.

"What was that all about?" Elizabeth asked, coming into Jessica's room again. She sat down on the bed. "I take it Lila didn't fall down dead with enthusiasm when you told her."

Jessica gave a little snort of disgust. "Lila can be such a pain sometimes. But she's coming anyway. I just wonder if—"

The telephone rang, and she snatched it up. "Hello?"

"Hi, can I speak to Elizabeth please?"

"Sure, she's right here. Who's calling?"

"This is Heather Sanford."

Jessica raised her eyebrows. Why would Heather be calling Elizabeth? she wondered. She covered the mouthpiece with her hand. "It's Heather Sanford."

Her sister's eyes widened in alarm. "Tell her I'm not home."

"But I just told her you were here!"

Elizabeth closed her eyes and sighed. Then she held out her hand for the phone with an air of resignation.

"Hi, Heather."

"Well, I'm in the middle of an art—" Jessica heard Elizabeth say a moment later.

Jessica looked down at her list again, trying to put a face to Heather's name. She was— Oh, right. Aaron Dallas's new girlfriend. A sophomore. Very stylish. Maybe she'd be a good person to add to the list.

She tugged on Elizabeth's sleeve. "Invite her to the party," she whispered.

Covering the mouthpiece, Elizabeth shook her head violently. "No!"

"Come on, Liz. You've got to!"

"I— Could you hold on a minute, Heather? Jessica, don't ask me to do that," she continued, holding her hand over the phone again.

"But, Liz, just this once, so I can get off to a good start. Please?" If she asked sincerely enough, Liz would give in. She always did. "Please, Lizzie?"

Elizabeth met her imploring eyes for a long, silent moment. Then she nodded.

"Sorry about that, Heather. My sister just

asked me something. She's giving a party here on Wednesday afternoon for Tofu-Glo."

"You have? Well, Jessica is a Tofu-Glo girl now, and she'd like you to come."

"You can?" Elizabeth winced. "Sure, I'll tell her. Listen, Heather, I really have to go now. Thanks for calling."

"You're welcome. Bye."

Elizabeth placed the receiver carefully on its cradle and turned to Jessica. "Well, she's coming," she said tersely.

"Thanks." Jessica looked closely at her twin. "You really didn't want her to come, did you?"

"It doesn't matter."

Jessica eyed her sister for a moment. It was obvious Elizabeth didn't like Heather. But just that once, it couldn't be that bad.

"Great," she said with a big smile. "This party is going to be *fantastic.*"

Five

"What time is it?" Jessica called out as she kicked the front door shut behind her.

She paused, shifting the two grocery bags in her arms. The house was very quiet.

"Liz?"

There was no answer. She rushed into the kitchen and began unpacking. Soon there was an assortment of health-food snacks piled on the table: soy chips, raisins, granola bars, toasted sunflower seeds, carob-covered nuts, natural vegetable juices, and mineral water.

Jessica eyed the snacks critically. They would be perfect, she decided. They'd help set the tone for the Tofu-Glo party. Getting her customers in the right frame of mind was important. It would make them more interested in the natural health and beauty products. The Tofu-Glo brochure had been emphatic about that.

"Urge your clients to pursue a pure, chemical-free life-style," Jessica repeated aloud. "It's the healthiest way to live."

A movement outside one plant-filled window caught her eye, and she strode quickly through the dining room to the patio door and threw it open.

"Liz! How can you just lie around sunbathing!" she demanded indignantly.

The Wakefields' backyard consisted of a sunny patio and a medium-size swimming pool. The Wakefields often used it for parties and barbecues.

Elizabeth sat up in the lounge chair near the pool. She shielded her eyes with one arm. "Oh, hi, Jess. Relax. People won't be here for another half hour! There's plenty of time!"

"Not if you're going to help me put all this food around."

Elizabeth stood up, pulled a top on over her turquoise maillot, and picked up her towel.

"OK, OK," she said with a smile.

As Elizabeth entered the kitchen, she saw the mounds of health food and raised her eyebrows. "How many people are you planning to feed?"

"I just want to be sure there's enough," Jessica said impatiently. She squeezed her hands together nervously.

Elizabeth said softly, "This really means a lot to you, doesn't it?"

"Are you kidding?" Jessica paused for a moment. "It's really important," she stated simply.

Elizabeth gave her an impulsive hug. "I'll go get dressed. And listen—everything is going to be great!"

Jessica felt a swell of pride and excitement. "You really think so?"

"Yeah. I do."

"Do I look OK?"

Elizabeth eyed her critically, a slight frown creasing her forehead. "Hmm . . ."

Jessica's heart sank. She flew through the house to the mirror in the front hall: denim miniskirt, open-necked white blouse, and blue sandals. "What's wrong?" she called. "Is it too unsophisticated, or something?"

Laughing and shaking her head, Elizabeth followed her twin. "I was just teasing you, Jess. I think you look fine."

Jessica breathed a sigh of relief and shook her head. "Don't ever do that to me again."

Elizabeth laughed again and ran upstairs.

Twenty minutes later Jessica placed the last bowl of carob-covered nuts on the coffee table and looked around. Everything seemed to be ready. There were extra chairs from all over the house, and she had run the vacuum cleaner over the rug quickly. She picked up a soy chip and nibbled it experimentally.

She frowned. "Tastes like—like salt," she decided, slightly disappointed.

Just then the door bell rang.

"Liz! Come on! They're here!"

She opened the door to the first group of girls—Dana Larson, her cousin Sally, and DeeDee Gordon—and for the next ten minutes she played hostess to perfection. Everyone had been given a hint that there was a special reason for the party, and that "all would be revealed" when everyone arrived.

As she stood at the door she could hear excited whispers behind her. Everyone was curious about her surprise. She grinned happily, pleased with the way she had set up her presentation. *They'll be hiring me as a Tofu-Glo consultant before I know it*, she told herself proudly.

Lila Fowler was the last to arrive. She stood in the doorway and shook her light-brown hair back over her shoulders. "Is this the Tupperware party?" She giggled as Jessica let her in.

"You be quiet," Jessica hissed, pulling her into the living room.

Lila chuckled and found a seat near Cara Walker, one of Jessica's best friends. Heather Sanford had planted herself next to Elizabeth and Enid as soon as she'd arrived, and kept asking if there was anything she could do to help. Her outfit made Jessica glad she'd be making a lot of money. Pretty soon she would be able to buy dozens of new outfits.

"Well, I guess you all want to know what this is all about," Jessica began, standing in the middle of the room. A row of expectant faces watched her, the eyes all politely fixed on her. She pushed a stray blond lock behind one ear. Never in her life had she been so excited and nervous. She hardly knew what to say.

Then she remembered the advice from her Tofu-Glo brochure: "Relax. Enjoy yourself. Knowing that these products are one-hundred-percent pure should set you and your client completely at ease. Remember, Tofu-Glo is good for you."

Feeling more confident, Jessica smiled and nodded. "Help yourself to those chips and things. There are nuts and seeds and stuff. And glasses of juice and mineral water. It's all completely pure and natural. Go ahead."

There was a brief rustling as the girls reached hesitantly for the snacks. But in a moment, all eyes were on Jessica again.

"I know it's a little unusual, but I'd like to talk to you about a company I recently found out about. They make beauty and health care products that are completely natural." She paused dramatically and looked at the expectant faces. "The company is called Tofu-Glo, and I'm a Tofu-Glo girl."

Murmurs of surprise greeted this announcement. Someone giggled. "What is it called?"

"Tofu-Glo," she repeated distinctly, letting the surprise sink in. She heard whispers of "Did you ever hear of it?" and "Sounds weird," then she continued.

"I'd like you all to try Tofu-Shampu, Tofu-Clean, Soya-Soft, and Soya-Life Dietary Supplement," Jessica said, putting a container of each on the coffee table. "These products are guaranteed to make your skin, your hair, your whole body look and feel great."

Her assurance grew as she described each of the products in detail. And she could tell her confidence was paying off. Every girl was listening with rapt attention.

Jessica thought, *This is even better than I expected*, as she paused to catch her breath.

"As I said, the main active ingredient in each of these things is soybeans, the same stuff those chips are made of."

"Does it taste the same?" Cara asked and giggled. She looked at the soy chip she had been nibbling.

Jessica smirked at her friend. "Actually, Cara, I haven't eaten the shampoo. But go ahead and taste it if you want."

A chorus of laughter boosted her confidence.

Across the room she caught Elizabeth's eye. Her twin was smiling at her, obviously proud. Jessica's heart soared.

"Anyway, soybeans are one of nature's miracles. And Tofu-Glo works so well I'm giving a money-back guarantee on these products." That was her own idea. She wondered briefly if she should make that kind of offer, but she was positive everyone would love the stuff.

"That's right," she went on. "If you don't like it, I'll buy it back from you. Any questions?"

Lois Waller, a shy, overweight girl whom Jessica had invited on the spur of the moment, raised her hand timidly. "Is the dietary supplement part of a diet plan?"

"No, no," Jessica said slowly. "It's a supplement, like taking vitamins. Only it's more than that."

Her mind raced as she tried to recall exactly what the brochure had said about it. She couldn't quite remember, so she decided to just reassure Lois anyway. It could clinch a sale. "But I suppose," she said with a playful smile, "as long as you use it, you're getting so much nutrition, you don't really have to eat. It's that good for you."

"Wow, that's great." Lois giggled and blushed slightly.

Another girl put up her hand.

"Yes, Maria?" Jessica asked, turning to the petite cheerleader.

Maria Santelli cleared her throat. "How about this Tofu-Shampu, Jess? I have to wash my hair after cheerleading practice, besides washing it every morning. Is it safe to use that often?"

"Sure! No problem."

"Sounds good," Maria decided. "I guess I'll give it a try."

Jessica glowed. "My first customer! So for you, the shampoo is free!" She turned to the rest of the girls. "Now, who's next?"

Hands shot up, and the girls started to press forward to place their orders. For the next fifteen minutes Jessica was surrounded by buyers eager for Tofu-Glo. The party was a stunning success.

Jessica caught Lila's eye and grinned. She almost wanted to stick her tongue out, but she figured that might be a bad idea. Besides, it looked as if Lila might buy some Tofu-Glo. So she just smiled.

"Hey, Julie," she said, pouncing on one of the members of Pi Beta Alpha, Julie Porter. "Why don't you get some for your sister, too? I'm sorry I couldn't invite her. I don't know where she hangs out these days."

Julie's face clouded with a quick flush of embarrassment. "Sure, I'll take another bottle of shampoo," she said, looking over her shoulder.

Anything to make a sale, Jessica told herself firmly. She knew Julie was embarrassed about her older sister, Johanna, because Johanna had dropped out of school the previous year. She still lived in Sweet Valley, but nobody ever heard about her anymore. A little twinge of guilt made Jessica pause for a moment, and she almost apologized to Julie. But the girl hurried away before she could say anything.

"Are you going to buy anything?" Elizabeth asked Enid quietly.

Enid shrugged. "I don't know. I never believe in these 'miracle' products. They always sound too good to be true. It's probably just another gimmick. Lord knows there are plenty of those around."

Elizabeth nodded. "I know. But just buy one thing, OK?" She met her friend's eyes. "It would really mean a lot to Jess."

"Ha! As if she'd even notice!"

"Well, just this once. Please?"

Enid rolled her eyes. "Oh, all right! I give in," she said, smiling. "What do you recommend?"

"Actually, I haven't tried any of it yet."

Elizabeth looked at her sister with affection. Her twin was still surrounded, answering questions and handing out Tofu-Glo products. "But it looks like the shampoo is selling pretty well. Why don't you try that."

"OK, Liz. But don't say I never did anything for you!"

"Go on." Still grinning, Elizabeth watched Enid join the group around Jessica. As she looked at the crowd, Heather Sanford detached herself and moved toward Elizabeth with an armload of Tofu-Glo products.

"I'm so glad you invited me," she said shoving jars and bottles into an oversize straw bag. She pushed a stray curl behind one ear and beamed at Elizabeth. "It was so much fun."

"I'm glad you had a good time," Elizabeth replied, smiling faintly. Heather had already thanked her several times. The girl had taken a seat next to her and made comments throughout Jessica's presentation, just as she had done at the movies on Friday night.

"Liz, I'm really sorry. I have to leave now. I have to meet Aaron after soccer practice. I'm sorry I have to go early."

Elizabeth felt a sense of relief, but she tried not to show it. "Oh, that's all right," she assured Heather, thinking that she must sound awfully phony. "I'm glad you could come."

Enid returned at that moment. Before she moved into Heather's line of sight, she crossed her eyes for a split second, staring at Heather's back. Elizabeth pressed her lips together to keep from laughing.

"Are you leaving, Heather?" Enid asked, smiling.

The girl nodded. "Yeah, I have to. But it was really fun talking to you, Enid."

Enid and Elizabeth exchanged glances. "Sure. Bye, Heather."

"I'll walk you to the door," Elizabeth offered, perfectly willing to speed up Heather's departure.

After a few more thank-yous, Heather finally left, and Elizabeth rejoined Enid in the living room.

"That girl is too much," Elizabeth said. "I mean, she's awfully sweet, but she's driving me crazy!"

She threw herself onto the couch, and Enid joined her. Soon a small group of girls were talking about school, and somehow the topic of the soccer finals came up.

"Please," Elizabeth pleaded with a groan. "Don't remind me of soccer, or Aaron Dallas, or Heather. I've had as much of those two as I can take right now."

Penny Ayala, editor-in-chief of *The Oracle*,

laughed sympathetically. "Sounds pretty serious, Liz."

"Honestly!" Shaking her head, Elizabeth recalled their embarrassing double date with vivid clarity. "What really drives me out of my mind more than anything though, is that she baby talks! And I *really* mean baby talk! We went out a week ago Friday, and Aaron was mad about something, as usual, and Heather tried to get him to cheer up. 'Oh, Aaron,' " she improvised. " 'Peez, don't be angway!' "

A round of laughter greeted her imitation. "I've heard her, too," DeeDee Gordon put in. "It's really amazing. I think she believes it's perfectly normal for a high-school student to sound like a three-year-old."

Elizabeth grinned, getting into the spirit of it. "What was it she said he was? Oh, right. 'Gwumpy.' "

There were more giggles, and Elizabeth got carried away. She thought about how Heather always overdressed for events, "An' I don' want you to be gwumpy, cause then nobody can tee my pwitty new cwose!"

"Liz! You're terrible!" Enid said, laughing but surprised that Elizabeth would make fun of someone.

Suddenly the dimple disappeared from Elizabeth's cheek. It was terrible. How could she make fun of Heather behind the girl's back? Sure, she was a bit of a nuisance, but still . . .

Now three of the girls were baby-talking about Tofu-Glo and exclaiming about how wonderful it would make them look. The whole group rocked with laughter each time one of them spoke. Elizabeth felt deeply ashamed of herself.

It wasn't that she was afraid that Heather would find out. The girl didn't seem to be very sensitive, and probably wouldn't even care. But she realized she was just being malicious—and Heather didn't deserve it.

She stood up abruptly. "I'll just take these out to the kitchen," she said in a tight voice as she picked up some empty bowls.

The laughter followed her as she left the living room.

Six

Heather Sanford put her oversize shoulder bag down on the steps of Sweet Valley High. She pulled her hairbrush out of her bag and began to brush her glossy curls. Then she took out a compact and looked at her reflection. After putting on more lipstick she put everything back in the bag and picked it up. She couldn't go to soccer practice looking as if she had just gotten off a roller coaster.

Looking good was important to her. She wasn't vain, just proud of her appearance. That was what had gotten her interested in fashion design in the first place. She had very definite ideas about what she wanted to wear, and if it wasn't possible to find it—well, then she just made it herself. Now she designed and sewed almost all her own clothes, and she was proud of her accomplishments.

She smoothed down her soft gray linen skirt, then began walking toward the field.

Now, off to see Aaron, she told herself, smiling. Thinking about Aaron always made her happy. He was a terrific guy, warm, funny, and generous, and she would never forget how he had taken the time to find out who she really was. If it weren't for his temper, things would be perfect.

But he got so angry sometimes, just the way his father did. She knew that Mr. Dallas was going through a nightmare with his divorce. And she couldn't always blame him for losing his temper. After all, for him to find out suddenly that his wife was leaving him and their son and moving across the country to live with another man— Well, that had to be pretty rough.

On the other hand, there were times, Heather reflected, when Mr. Dallas was out of control. She shivered as she recalled seeing him yell at Aaron one night after Aaron had made a perfectly innocent mistake. And his yelling had gotten to be a common occurrence, too. Just about every time Aaron did anything, his father would yell at him.

Like father, like son, she thought, shaking her head. So, she had to try to calm Aaron down whenever he got upset about something. Like the other night.

She blushed suddenly. She had seen the look on Elizabeth Wakefield's face, and she didn't blame her. It was embarrassing to talk baby talk, but Aaron thought it was cute, and he usually relaxed when she did it.

If it weren't for Elizabeth, she wouldn't mind. But it was obvious that Elizabeth didn't like her very much, and she knew the baby talk hadn't helped. But what could she do? She had tried to make Elizabeth like her, but it didn't seem to make any impression.

Heather sighed. She was sorry about Elizabeth because she really liked and respected her. But, well, Elizabeth Wakefield was so poised and smart, Heather felt that she herself always ended up sounding dumb and immature when she talked to the older girl. No wonder Elizabeth didn't want to be her friend.

She looked quickly around the soccer field and caught Aaron's eye. He jogged over to her and gave her a quick kiss on the cheek.

"Remember what we talked about?" she asked, looking anxiously up into his eyes.

With an impatient glance over his shoulder, Aaron shook his head. "Don't worry, Heather. I'm not going to argue with anybody today, OK? Just don't worry about it."

Biting back her reply, Heather nodded mutely. "Are you sure?"

"Yes, I'm sure. I've got to go."

She watched him run back onto the field

and then turned to climb up the bleachers. For all his confidence, she wasn't so sure. More often than not he got into arguments instead of avoiding them. And she didn't know how to help him at all.

"Hey, soccer star!"

Elizabeth poked her head around Jeffrey's locker door and grinned impishly.

His eyes sparkled with laughter. "Ah! My biggest fan. You're going to show your undying loyalty by coming to practice today, aren't you?" he asked, closing the locker with a snap. "Guaranteed to surprise and delight you."

"Actually, yes, but only because I'm so dedicated to my work."

They started walking down the hall, and Jeffrey looked at her with an amused but puzzled frown. "What's that supposed to mean?"

Elizabeth giggled. "I'm covering practice today for an article," she explained, taking her boyfriend's hand as they walked. Elizabeth wrote the "Eyes and Ears" column for *The Oracle*, the school newspaper, as well as articles on many different topics. "I figure that since the big game is next week, there could be a real human interest story in it. You know—hopes and fears—all of that juicy stuff."

"Hopes and fears! Just hopes this time, Liz." Jeffrey released her hand to put his arm across her shoulders, and he gave her a squeeze. "We're going to win this year. I know it. Especially with Aaron as a starter. He's really fantastic."

Elizabeth said unenthusiastically, "You're right about that. He is good."

Jeffrey stopped. "You really don't like Aaron, do you?" he asked point-blank.

Her heart gave a painful lurch. "It's not that, really. It's just— I wish he didn't have such a short fuse. He used to be such a nice guy. Everybody liked him."

"But I've told you, Liz. He's really having a rough time with his dad. Underneath he's still the same nice guy."

Elizabeth shook her head. She knew enough not to start debating the subject again. Besides, they had reached the locker-room door, and it was time for Jeffrey to get ready for practice. She made an effort to get rid of her gloomy thoughts. She smiled up at Jeffrey. "Maybe you're right. See you later, OK?"

"You can count on it," Jeffrey said softly, looking down into her eyes.

She grinned, not wanting to leave him. "Hey! Do you think I could come in, too?" She nodded toward the locker room door.

"See you later," Jeffrey repeated firmly. He

gave her a playful shove toward the outside door, and Elizabeth laughed.

"OK, just checking."

As she made her way out to the soccer field, Elizabeth mentally reviewed the situation for her story. The championship game against their rival, Big Mesa, was exactly one week away, next Thursday. That meant tensions had to be mounting, special strategies mapped out. She could interview some of the players, she decided. And Coach Horner.

Glancing into the bleachers, she saw Heather Sanford sitting about halfway up. Elizabeth smiled, waved and then sat down purposefully on the bottom step. She pulled out her notebook. From the corner of her eye she saw Heather rise uncertainly, and she held her breath. But the girl sat down again. Elizabeth heaved a sigh of relief and pulled out a pen.

As she planned out her article, the players arrived on the field and practice began. It was mostly boring drill to begin with, and Elizabeth used the time to work on creating a background of anticipation and suspense. She wrote a quick summary of Sweet Valley High's soccer record and set the stage for the present year. She had written several paragraphs when the soccer team divided to play a practice game.

That was the moment Elizabeth had been

waiting for. She was hoping to draw brief profiles of as many players as she could, and she wanted to study their styles, if it was possible. But as she watched the game, she decided that either all of them were very good, or her eye wasn't practiced enough.

There was only one player who stood out. Aaron Dallas seemed to be everywhere with the ball. For a few moments Elizabeth forgot the impatience and anxiety she felt about Aaron and let herself admire the way he played.

"You're good, Aaron," she said softly with ungrudging respect. "You're very good."

It occurred to her then that since he was co-captain and star of the team, Aaron should take a lead role in her article, too. As a reporter, she had to be objective, so no matter what she felt about him personally, she knew he deserved the attention.

Her pen flew across the page as she wrote a portrait of Aaron. She looked up again, searching the field. There was Jeffrey, doing his usual great job, she noticed, smiling with pride. And there was Aaron, carefully bringing the ball downfield into position.

He was keeping a wary eye on Jeffrey to his right, guarding against his friend's attempted steals. Then all of a sudden, Brad Tomasi cut in from Aaron's left and stole the ball neatly away. Aaron tripped as Brad cut him off, and the team's star player sprawled forward onto his hands and knees.

He was up again instantly, racing after Brad. Elizabeth assumed he must be trying to get the ball back. But when Aaron caught up to the other boy, he tackled him.

"You jerk!" he screamed, pummeling Brad's face. "You nearly broke my leg back there!"

There was a stunned pause. The players all looked as though they had been turned to stone. The coach's whistle began to screech, and they all surged forward to break up the fight.

Jeffrey struggled to hold Aaron off Brad as the others helped the stunned boy to his feet.

"Let me go! Let me go!" Aaron continued yelling, and he lunged forward, nearly breaking free from Jeffrey's grip.

Blood was streaming from Brad's nose. The coach examined him carefully before sending him to the nurse's office with two boys to help him. Finally he turned slowly to Aaron Dallas, and his voice was icy.

"I ought to punch you out for that one, Dallas, but I'd be arrested."

Aaron's chest was heaving, and he glared at the coach defiantly. "He's a clumsy idiot!" he shouted. "He deliberately tripped me. Everyone saw him do it."

"And everyone saw you attack him," the coach retorted, his face becoming as red as Aaron's. "There is absolutely no excuse for what you just pulled, Dallas. I'm putting you on notice: one more fight, one more shout out of you—anywhere in this town—and you're off the team. Do I make myself perfectly clear?"

"But you can't do that!" Aaron said sullenly, his eyes blazing.

The coach's voice dropped then, becoming very low and intense. "I will do exactly what I choose and I do not choose to tolerate that kind of infantile, prima donna behavior on my team. So you are hereby suspended until Tuesday. And," he added, silencing Aaron's hot protest, "if you want to play in Thursday's game, you will *enjoy* being suspended."

The two stared at each other. The air was charged with tension.

"OK now, *move*! All of you!"

As Coach Horner bellowed at the team, Aaron stalked off the field. Jeffrey stared after him, a stricken expression on his handsome face. There was a quick patter of feet on the bleachers as Heather Sanford climbed down to chase after Aaron. She caught up with him and began gesturing and talking.

Elizabeth's heart was thumping painfully in her chest, and her cheeks were hot. Aaron's outburst was utterly horrifying. That anyone could lose control of his temper so quickly and totally was frightening. There was no doubt in her mind that Aaron was in serious trouble and he needed help soon. There was no telling what he might do.

She looked unhappily down the field to where Jeffrey was. He must see it now, she told herself. Nobody could be that loyal. Even as she stared at him, Jeffrey looked up, and their eyes met. Then he turned away quickly.

A pain in her fingers startled Elizabeth, and she looked down to see that she was gripping her pen so hard that her knuckles were white. She shook her hand and stared bleakly at the notebook on her knees.

So much for that article, she told herself grimly. Now that the star player was suspended, she could hardly write an upbeat, optimistic story about Sweet Valley High's chances of winning the regional title.

But she did have an article to write, she realized. It wasn't going to make anyone happy, but she couldn't ignore what had just happened. She was a reporter, and she had to tell the story as she saw it. And she had just seen Aaron Dallas attack a teammate for accidentally knocking him down in the heat of the action. And that, she told herself with a sinking heart, was not the kind of scoop she wanted to have.

The article would appear in the next *Oracle*, which came out the following week on Monday. "And after that," she muttered, "I'll be lucky if Jeffrey ever speaks to me again."

For a moment she hesitated. *It seems so unfair to Aaron,* she told herself with a guilty pang. *He's having such a hard time. Should I really mention it?* But then she shook her head. It wasn't as if she were deliberately picking on him. She just couldn't ignore what had happened. Could she?

She turned to a fresh page in her notebook and, gritting her teeth, began writing.

Tensions are mounting for the soccer finals this week, and the level of excitement is soaring. All our players are in fine form, but it looks as though they're starting to feel the heat.

Aaron Dallas, co-captain and acknowledged star of the team, began an unprovoked attack on a fellow player, teammate Brad Tomasi, at practice last week.

The fight was quickly brought to a halt by other team members, but Brad had already suffered a bloody nose.

Coach Horner sent the student to the nurse's office. Aaron Dallas came away from the brawl with a warning: another outburst and he would be removed from the team. He was suspended from practice for a few days.

The team is gearing up for the big Big Mesa showdown. Coach Horner seems to be . . .

Aaron's hands shook as he changed out of his soccer uniform. *The nerve of that guy!* he fumed. *Where does he get off suspending me?*

He slammed the door of his locker shut, and it bounced open again. He slammed it again, and it still refused to close.

"Dammit!" he yelled, dangerously close to tears.

He sat down abruptly on a bench and buried his face in his hands. Everything was against him that day, he thought bitterly. Lately it was always like that. He always was blamed for everyone else's mistakes.

Why do people do this? he wondered in silent anguish. Cutting him off on purpose, humiliating him in front of the whole school, getting him in trouble—getting divorced!

With a wracking, painful sob, Aaron began to cry. It all came back to him, the afternoon he had been trying to blot out of his memory. He had come home from school and was surprised to see his father's car in the driveway. Without being told, he had known something was wrong.

And then inside, he had seen his mother and father sitting at the kitchen table, their faces stern and bitter. "Your mother has decided to go to New York," his dad had said. "And we think all we can do now is get a divorce. I'm sorry, son."

His mother had tried to smile at him, he remembered. But it only came out as a sort of crooked grimace. And then she had gone, leaving him with his father and the terrible arguments.

His breathing became labored as he realized just how helpless he was. Nothing he could do would make all his problems disappear, make things the way they were before. Sometimes he felt as if he were drowning, and there was nothing to hold on to, nothing stable and reliable that he could count on.

"It's not my fault!" he choked out, his throat constricting with hot tears. "Everyone makes me so mad! What do they expect from me? It's not my fault!"

Seven

"Hi! My name is Jessica Wakefield. I'm your Tofu-Glo girl."

"Hello. I'm your Tofu-Glo girl, Jessica Wakefield."

Jessica gave her reflection her most winning smile and tried again.

"Hello! I'd like to talk to you about Tofu-Glo. I think you'll love it."

The blue-green eyes meeting hers smiled back. "Oh, won't you come in? I'm very interested."

She giggled at her own silliness and gave herself one last critical survey in the mirror. That afternoon she was going to start selling Tofu-Glo around the neighborhood, and her spirits were high.

She hummed a little as she left the bathroom. That party two days before had been incredible. Not in her wildest dreams had she expected to sell so much to her friends. At least a third of the boxes were empty.

On the threshold of her room she paused. There was that odor again, she thought. She had smelled it earlier in the day. *I hope Prince Albert didn't hide something in my room*, she thought, wrinkling her nose. She strode to the window to let in some fresh air. *I'll look around later*, she decided.

She regarded the stack of cartons in the corner. How much should she take? She couldn't very well drag a bunch of boxes around town, but she had her car, so at least she didn't have to go on foot."

"I'll take one box of each," she said out loud. "And when I run out, I'll just take orders." With that optimistic plan, Jessica proceeded to carry one box each of Tofu-Shampu, Tofu-Clean, Soya-Soft, and Soya-Life down to the red convertible.

Soon she was spinning along the quiet suburban streets of Sweet Valley. She had already decided to start with people who didn't know her. After all, she wanted people to buy her products because she was a good salesperson, not because they knew who she was.

She pulled into a street, Moonglow Terrace. That seemed like a good omen, having "glow" in the name. That was where she would start. She pulled the Fiat to the curb at the first house and grabbed her canvas bag with a sample of each product.

"Here goes," she whispered, squaring her shoulders and fixing a big smile on her face.

"Hi! My name is Jessica Wakefield, and I'm your Tofu-Glo girl," she chirped to the pleasant, middle-aged woman who answered the door. "Can I show you some of our health and beauty products today?"

"Well . . ." The woman smiled uncertainly and glanced over her shoulder into the house.

"It'll only take a few moments, ma'am. I'm sure you'll be very interested." Jessica smiled harder, her eyes bright.

Finally the woman nodded her head and smiled back. "All right, dear. Come on in."

"This is a lovely house," Jessica remembered to say. "My mom couldn't have done a better job, and she's an interior designer."

The woman stopped and turned around with a surprised smile on her lips. "Did you say your name is Wakefield?"

"Yes."

"Well, what a coincidence." She laughed. "Your mother did do my house! She's Alice Wakefield, right?"

Jessica couldn't believe her luck. The woman wasn't a stranger, but if Jessica played her cards right, she knew she could definitely make a sale. "That's right," she said with a big grin. "I guess we have the same good taste!"

"Well, come right on into the living room, Jessica. I'm Mrs. Bowen." She settled herself on the sofa and offered Jessica a mint. "And now let's see what you've got there, dear."

With Mrs. Bowen listening politely, Jessica reeled off her well-rehearsed presentation about Tofu-Glo, stressing that people these days were making the "natural choice."

"And my mom uses it, too," she said, thinking that one little lie couldn't hurt.

"Hmm. Well, why don't I just take one of each, Jessica. How would that be? And have a mint," she added, pushing the dish forward again.

Jessica tried not to shout with glee. "That's wonderful, Mrs. Bowen. And I also offer a money-back guarantee."

"I'm sure that won't be necessary, dear. Now how much does that come to?"

With a deft, professional manner, Jessica wrote up a receipt and took a check from Mrs. Bowen. she couldn't stop grinning as she preceded her customer to the front door.

"Thank you very much, Mrs. Bowen. I hope you like it."

Mrs. Bowen beamed at her. "I'm sure I will, sweetie. Now be sure to tell everyone on the street I'm a customer of yours. And give my best to your mother."

"I will." Jessica waved as she got into her car and drove to the next house. Her heart was soaring. What unbelievable luck—the whole product line on her first try!

"You're a born salesperson, Jessica," she told herself confidently. "This is turning out to be the best idea I ever had."

At the next three houses, Mrs. Bowen's reference opened all the doors, and Jessica made three more sales. Her confidence rose every minute. Before long, phrases like "natural toning process" and "protein enhancers" were rolling off her tongue as easily as her own name.

It wasn't until the fifth stop of the afternoon that she was stumped.

"May I try some first?" the lady repeated.

Jessica shrugged. No one else had asked to try it first. But—well, she couldn't see why she shouldn't.

"Oh, of course," she replied with a start. She smiled hesitantly at the hatchet-faced woman. The woman did not smile back.

As she fumbled with the jar of Soya-Soft, Jessica felt herself blushing. It finally came loose after an embarrassing struggle. And then Jessica recoiled. So did the customer.

"Is that smell from the cream?" she demanded, her face showing clear signs of doubt.

"Oh, well— You see—" Jessica's mind raced. "They don't put in artificial fragrances, you see . . ." She faltered and then regained her confidence. "The smell goes away after you use it."

The woman regarded the open jar with unveiled skepticism.

"Go ahead. Try some," Jessica urged desperately. "Please?"

"Well, all right. If you're sure the smell goes away?"

"Yes, yes, I'm sure."

Taking a deep breath, the lady reached out and scooped a little dab of Soya-Soft cream out of the jar; then she began to massage it into her hands.

There was a tense silence as she rubbed and rubbed her hands, waiting for the cream to soak into her skin. The woman raised her eyes briefly to Jessica's face and then looked down at her hands. The cream just lay there like a coating of smelly grease.

Jessica stared in disbelief. There must be something wrong with the woman's skin. Whoever heard of skin that wouldn't absorb moisturizing cream?

"Don't you like it?" Jessica asked timidly.

The woman glared at her and held up her

hands as though they were contaminated. "I think I'll go wash this off. You can show yourself out, I'm sure."

Her cheeks burning, Jessica hastily repacked her samples and fled. When she got behind the steering wheel, she drew a deep breath. She was shaken up, not because she had any doubts about Tofu-Glo, but because her fantastic winning streak was over so soon.

"That's enough for today," she decided, putting the car into gear. "Tomorrow I'll go out again." A few minutes later she was back home and walking through the house to see whether anybody was around.

"Hi," she said wearily as she sat down at the kitchen table.

Alice Wakefield turned from the counter, where she was cutting up vegetables for dinner. "Hi, sweetheart. Did you have many takers?"

"Yeah. It was OK. Oh, and I sold some stuff to a lady you did a house for, Mrs. Bowen."

"Oh, really? She's a very nice woman. I enjoyed working for her."

The memory of her first easy conquest cheered Jessica up. "She bought the whole line," she said happily. "And she kept offering me mints!"

Her mother laughed. "She was always doing that to me, too. I—"

The phone rang, and Jessica reached for it.

"Hi, Jess? It's me, Cara."

"Hi. What's up?"

There was a pause before Cara Walker continued. "Well, you know how I bought some shampoo from you on Wednesday, right?"

A warning bell went off in Jessica's head. "Yeah," she said guardedly.

"Well, I tried it this afternoon, and—well, Jess! It won't rinse out of my hair! Jess?"

"I'm here. What do you mean it won't rinse out?" Jessica met her mother's widened eyes across the room and made a sour face.

"I mean it won't rinse out," Cara repeated sharply. "I tried for half an hour! And it won't come out! My hair is totally disgusting!"

Jessica swallowed hard. "But, Cara—"

"And I'm supposed to go out with Steven tonight, but obviously I can't now!"

Jessica winced. The twins' older brother dated Cara and often came home weekends to see her. He wasn't going to appreciate being stood up.

"So what about that money-back guarantee, Jess?"

"*What?*"

"The money-back guarantee. You said if I'm not satisfied with—"

"I know what I said," Jessica snapped. She did some rapid calculation. "Oh, all right. I'll give you your money back. And I'll explain to Steven, too."

"Well, thanks, Jessica. Bye."

"Bye." She slowly replaced the phone on its hook and turned to face her mother. "Cara didn't like the shampoo. She said it didn't rinse out of her hair."

"Oh, honey. That's too bad." Mrs. Wakefield shook her head sympathetically. "Did you have the same problem?"

"Well, actually, Mom, I haven't tried it."

Her mother looked at her in surprise. "You haven't? For goodness sake, Jessica. Why not?"

The beginnings of a blush crept up Jessica's cheeks, and she looked away.

"Well, you've tested the other things, haven't you?" Mrs. Wakefield paused ominously. "Haven't you?"

"Not exactly."

"Oh, Jessica! Honestly! I'm surprised at you. How can you sell those products if you haven't tried them on yourself first?"

"But, Mom!" Jessica squirmed in her seat.

Her mother turned away, and her voice sounded disappointed. "Well, I think you'd better go upstairs right now and try each one of those products."

"Oh, all right."

"And, Jess, I think Prince Albert might have dragged something under your bed. A piece of food or something. There's some kind of a smell."

Jessica stomped up the stairs, her thoughts in a turmoil. Why did Cara have to ruin her good mood? At the doorway of her room she halted. That smell. It was much more noticeable now, but she just ignored it.

Still fuming, Jessica extracted a bottle of Tofu-Shampu and a bottle of Tofu-Clean and strode into the bathroom. With dark thoughts directed at Cara, she climbed into the shower to wash her hair.

The shampoo, when she opened it, had as strong and as foul an odor as the Soya-Soft cream. But she gritted her teeth and poured some out anyway. *It lathers just fine*, she thought. *So what's the problem? A little smell? Big deal.*

She stepped under the steaming rush of water to rinse the shampoo out. Her hands moved quickly across her scalp, pushing the suds out with the water. And more suds. She kept rinsing and rinsing—and still her hair felt soapy.

Jessica's heart sank as she finally realized it was not coming out. After turning off the taps, Jessica stepped out of the shower and wrapped a towel around herself. She rubbed her hair with another towel. Her hair was sticking together. "So something's wrong with the shampoo," she mumbled. "I can live with that."

On the edge of the sink was the bottle of Tofu-Clean. Jessica regarded it skeptically. Then, steeling her nerves, she began to wash her face, alert for any sign that it would not rinse out. It had the same offensive smell, but with a few splashes of water, it came right off.

"No problem," she said, looking happily at her dripping face in the mirror. But as the moisture evaporated, Jessica's skin began to feel tight and irritated. She wiggled her jaw, beginning to worry.

With every second the stinging sensation increased, and her skin began to turn a mottled red. She leaned over the sink in panic, splashing her face with cold water. Finally the stinging subsided, but her face was bright pink.

"Oh, no!" she groaned. "I look terrible!" Immediately after that she realized she couldn't let anybody see her like that! Neil Freemount, a boy she dated occasionally, had asked her to go to a movie that night. But she'd rather die than appear in public right then.

Elizabeth poked her head into the bathroom. "What's the smell? Jess, what happened to your face?"

Whirling around, Jessica thrust the bottle of Tofu-Clean into her twin's hand "This! This is what happened! I can't believe it!"

"And your hair! Did the Tofu-Glo do that, too?"

Jessica nodded mutely.

"Oh, wow." Elizabeth shook her head. "That's awful, Jess. I'm really sorry."

"You're sorry! You don't look like this!" Jessica wailed, holding out one stringy, sticky lock of dull blond hair. "It won't come out, my face looks like a tomato, and I have a date tonight," she finished.

Elizabeth opened her mouth to speak and then paused as if choosing her words carefully. "Maybe you ought to just stay home tonight," she suggested as delicately as possible.

With angry tears in her eyes, Jessica nodded. "You don't have to be so polite, Liz. Just say it. I look like the bride of Frankenstein! I'm going to call Neil and tell him I have the plague."

The phone rang, startling both girls. "I'll get it," Elizabeth offered, moving past Jessica.

"It's for you, Jess," she called. "A Mrs. Bowen. She says she wants her money back."

Jessica winced and walked into her room like a prisoner heading for the electric chair. Mrs. Bowen stated kindly but firmly that she was dissatisfied with Tofu-Glo and would like to return the products.

"All of them?" Jessica whispered, close to tears.

"All of them."

The evening got progressively worse. Before dinner even started Jessica took five more calls from unhappy customers. And during dinner Steven kept asking her what she had done to Cara.

"And what's this smell?" her father asked, a puzzled frown on his face.

Jessica sank lower in her chair as the phone rang again.

"I can't talk to anyone else today," she moaned, her head in her hands. "Please!"

"I told you you should do some in-depth research," Mr. Wakefield reminded her.

"Ned, please! I don't think that's very helpful right now." Mrs. Wakefield patted Jessica's hand softly and gave her a rueful smile.

"Why would you want to sell Cara tofu to put on her hair?" Steven asked for the seventh time, annoyed and puzzled. "I don't get it."

Prince Albert appeared suddenly, a container of Soya-Life held gingerly in his mouth. He dropped it reproachfully in the doorway and began to bark at it.

Jessica burst into tears and fled from the room.

Eight

On Monday morning Elizabeth got dressed with a fair amount of trepidation. Her article on Aaron Dallas's fight would appear in that day's *Oracle*.

Deep in thought, she made her way downstairs. But the smell from Jessica's room intruded. It was too potent to ignore.

"I want that Tofu-Glo out of the house and into the garage this afternoon, Jessica," her mother was saying at the foot of the stairs.

Jessica nodded glumly and cast Elizabeth a look of appeal as the sound of Prince Albert's angry barking reached them from upstairs. It had finally become clear that it was the Tofu-Glo that was causing the nauseating smell. It seemed to be rotting in Jessica's room.

"Come on, Jess," Elizabeth said. "Let's have breakfast. I'd like to get to school early."

For the whole ride to school, Jessica bewailed her bad fortune. Practically every one of her customers had called by the end of the week-end, requesting her money back. The Tofu-Glo had turned into a mess of stinking goo in the bottles and jars.

"It's just not fair," she complained bitterly. "Why do these things always happen to me?"

Elizabeth didn't answer. There wasn't any-thing she could say, she knew. Once Jessica was in a miserable mood, there was no point in even trying to cheer her up.

Besides, Elizabeth was too preoccupied with her own worries to give Jessica her full atten-tion. The closer they drew to school, the more she regretted having written the article. It wasn't that she thought anyone would be mad at her—anyone but Aaron and, maybe, Jeffrey.

But that year's soccer finals were of para-mount importance to the school, and she had thrown a very wet blanket over them. On the other hand, maybe the article would do some good, maybe it would finally bring Aaron to his senses. Maybe he needed to see his ac-tions described in black and white.

"Boy, are you asking for it," Enid mur-mured as she saw Elizabeth at her locker at lunchtime. "You really know how to 'win friends and influence people,' as the saying goes. Do you think Aaron's going to strangle you or shoot you?"

Elizabeth smiled at her friend. "I think I'll probably be dog meat by the end of the day," she said, nodding toward a group of students reading *The Oracle*, which had just come out. "Maybe I should think about moving to the North Pole."

"They don't care, believe me. But maybe Aaron will finally see what a jerk he's been," Enid suggested with a wry smile. "He's the only one who's really going to be upset about that story."

"I hope you're right. I guess I'll know soon enough. I'm supposed to have lunch with Jeffrey. Want to join us?"

"No, thanks," Enid said. "Let me know what Jeffrey has to say, though, OK?"

"Sure," Elizabeth said, taking her lunch bag out of her locker.

Elizabeth and Jeffrey had arranged to eat outside under one of the trees on the front lawn. As soon as Elizabeth saw Jeffrey, she knew something was very wrong.

"I don't get it," he said, his expression sad. "Why did you have to write that article?"

"Because I'm a reporter."

"But you're also supposed to be Aaron's friend! Come on, Liz. He's my best friend. That should count for something, shouldn't it?"

Elizabeth fought to keep her voice steady. She had thought Jeffrey would be a little upset, but she hoped he would try to understand. "I can't let my personal relationships get in the way of a story, Jeffrey. You know that."

"Oh, Liz, come on! Stop pulling that 'just the facts' stuff, OK? There wasn't any reason to single out Aaron about that fight. He had a good—"

"A good excuse?" Elizabeth cut in, her eyes blazing. "Jeffrey, Aaron got knocked down. So what? You guys are out there playing soccer, not Chinese checkers! I mean, what does he expect?"

"What you don't seem to understand, Liz, is how important Thursday's game is. We can't win it without Aaron, and you sound like he doesn't deserve to be on the team at all!"

"Well, maybe he doesn't!" she retorted angrily. "I think it's incredible that you keep defending him." She stared at Jeffrey, her heart beating. "Aaron loses his temper, and you always run to his rescue!"

Jeffrey was breathing heavily. "Well, he had every reason to be mad. And now he's even madder. He was so ticked off when he read your article he nearly hit me!"

Her eyes widened, and for a moment Elizabeth was speechless. "Did you hear yourself?" she said finally. "Doesn't it strike you as pretty crazy that he almost hit you? Don't you think there's anything wrong with that?"

Jeffrey looked away. "All I know is, my best friend is hardly speaking to me. And believe me," he added with a bitter laugh, "he doesn't want to see you. He said he won't go to the beach with us next weekend, for obvious reasons."

The words stung, but Jeffrey's tone was even worse. Elizabeth wished she could see Aaron right then so she could tell him off. She held him entirely to blame for causing this argument.

Swallowing with difficulty, she turned away. "I did what I thought was right," she said finally.

"Well, I'm going to find Aaron and try to apologize," Jeffrey replied curtly.

She heard him walk away, and her hand went to her trembling chin. She and Jeffrey had argued before, but never like that! How could Jeffrey be so blind? She wanted to scream.

Feeling as though she had just aged fifty years, Elizabeth walked to a trash container and threw away her unopened lunch. Then she sat down under a tree and closed her eyes, trying to control herself. She made herself breathe slowly and evenly, and finally she relaxed a little. Then she opened her eyes, and her heart started racing again. Heather Sanford was heading straight for her!

Oh, no! she moaned silently. *Not this. Not on top of everything else!*

But Heather obviously didn't pick up Elizabeth's unspoken distress signal. She looked over her shoulder once and sat down on the grass, a tentative smile on her lips.

"Before you say anything, Heather, I'm not sorry I wrote that article, and I'd write it again. That's just how I feel."

Heather's eyes widened. "But, Liz, I wanted to tell you—I—I'm glad, well, not really glad, but . . ." Her voice trailed off.

Elizabeth stared at her.

"I mean, I think you did the right thing, too. That article, I mean."

Elizabeth still stared speechlessly.

"What I'm trying to say," Heather continued, becoming ruffled by Elizabeth's silence, "is that you were right to tell what really happened."

Her mind in a whirl, Elizabeth nodded. "You do? I mean, you really think so?"

Heather nodded, obviously unaware that she had just sent Elizabeth into a tailspin.

"Why?" Elizabeth prodded, trying to recover from the shock of finding Heather Sanford, of all people, on her side.

Blushing, Heather looked over her shoulder again. "Aaron had no right to hit Brad," she began, her voice low but firm. "I was really upset that he did it."

"I didn't realize you'd see it that way."

He had no right," she repeated. "And I almost hope he does get kicked off the team! Maybe then he'll see what he's doing to himself."

She stopped suddenly, as if surprised by her own vehemence, and began to cry. "He won't even admit he's got a problem," she choked out, pleating and unpleating the skirt of her dress as she continued. "Maybe getting himself kicked off the team would make him realize his temper is out of control."

Elizabeth's heart softened as she listened to the girl. It was obvious that Heather loved Aaron, but knew that Aaron's anger was all out of proportion.

With growing admiration, Elizabeth tried to comfort Heather as well as she could. "Have you tried talking to him about it?" she asked gently.

Heather sniffed. "Yes. But he just says, 'Well you're the only one who thinks so,' or 'It's perfectly normal to get angry,' or something like that."

The argument with Jeffrey came back to Elizabeth. "And I guess it doesn't help when his best friend keeps telling him he's right." She shook her head. "I'm really sorry, Heather."

"Oh, Liz! It's not your fault Jeffrey's so loyal."

Well, I still—" She broke off. She had tried, many times, to get Jeffrey to see that something was wrong with his friend. "I guess he can't admit it, either."

"I know. I didn't want to at first. I kept making excuses for him. But, Liz! You should see his father get mad!" The girl shuddered at the memory. "This whole divorce thing is driving them both crazy. Not that that's an excuse," she added quickly. "It's just the reason."

There was a short, contemplative silence while both girls considered the situation. After a few moments Heather collected herself and smiled sheepishly.

"Look what I'm doing to this dress." She laughed ruefully, looking at the crumpled material in her fist. "And I only finished it yesterday."

Elizabeth looked at Heather, surprised. "Did you make that yourself?"

"Yes."

"Do you make all your own clothes?" she asked, as Heather's statement about wanting to enter a fashion institute came back to her. She was angry at her own insensitivity.

"Well, almost all of them. The ones I design I do. I don't think there's anything very original in the stores around here." She looked down at her dress. "Do you like it?"

"Do I like it?" Elizabeth laughed. The dress, of pale peach cotton, fell gracefully from a dropped waist. A collar made of dozens of overlapping "petals" in white and pink added a lovely, flowerlike quality to the otherwise simple design. "It's gorgeous!"

Heather smiled. "Thanks. It took me forever to cut all these out!"

The two girls smiled at each other for a moment. Elizabeth suddenly realized that they had more in common than she had expected.

"Well, I'd better go find Aaron," Heather said, picking up her books. "He's not going to be exactly thrilled when he finds out I'm on your side."

Elizabeth put her hand on Heather's arm. "Don't tell him if you don't want to. I mean, don't do it for me."

Heather shook her head. "No, I have to tell him. But don't be surprised if we don't see each other very much for a while. He'll be pretty angry with you."

Shaking her head, Elizabeth answered,

"Well, this time I don't blame him! I guess I would be, too."

Both girls smiled. Then Heather stood up. "Well, bye, Liz."

"Bye."

Elizabeth watched the other girl walk away. How incredible that Heather had turned out to be on her side! she thought, shaking her head.

She realized guiltily that she had underestimated the younger girl. All her attention to Aaron was supportive and caring, not blind adoration. And the obsession about clothes? Elizabeth could kick herself for being so prejudiced. It was obvious that Heather was an interesting, creative girl who loved to talk about fashion design. That was understandable.

Elizabeth recalled again Heather telling her she wanted to study at a fashion institute. *But you were too superior to take her seriously*, she scolded herself. *Some objective reporter you are. Can't even tell when a person is honest and interesting. What a first-class snob!*

Heather was just the sort of person Elizabeth would like to know better. And it wasn't just because Heather took her side, Elizabeth decided. It was *why* Heather took her side.

But now it looked as though she and Heather wouldn't get the chance. Aaron was not going to forget her article in a hurry, and it would only put Heather in an awkward position if she and Elizabeth tried to be friendly.

The sun beat down on the grass, and students passed back and forth across the lawn. Elizabeth stayed under the tree until lunch was over and then got ready for her next class.

"What a day," she said with a sigh. "And it's not over yet!"

A few students continued to look indignant when Elizabeth caught their eyes. But there were plenty of others who either didn't care or actively supported her position. It was reassuring to know that she wasn't alone. But the tension she felt around her finally got her down. At the end of her last class, Elizabeth sought out Mr. Collins, the adviser to *The Oracle* and her favorite teacher.

"Ever feel like you've been accused of being a party pooper?" she asked, setting down her books on the English teacher's desk.

He looked grave, but his eyes twinkled. "Cutting down the star soccer player?" he asked. "Sounds like a bad case of no-school-spiritits."

Elizabeth laughed. "You're not kidding. But, really, do you think I should have softened my article somehow?" She frowned. She did have school spirit. That was why she hated to see Aaron shame their soccer team. "I don't know. Maybe I was too harsh."

There was silence as Mr. Collins regarded her thoughtfully. He leaned back in his chair and toyed with a pencil. "Liz, why did you join the newspaper staff?"

"Because I wanted to write," she said simply.

"What was it you wanted to write about?"

She thought a moment. "The world, I guess, as I see it."

"And this article," Roger Collins continued, nudging the paper with his pencil. "Is this as you saw it?"

"Yes," Elizabeth stated firmly.

He chuckled. "Liz, why are we having this conversation?"

His eyes twinkled again, and Elizabeth grinned. "Maybe I needed a little positive reinforcement from an authority figure."

"Oh, please! Never call me that!"

She laughed. Going to Mr. Collins was always the right thing to do. No matter what her dilemma, he was always helpful. And he usually helped her by making her figure out the answer herself.

"OK." She turned to go and looked back. "Thanks."

He winked. "Anytime, Liz."

As she made her way home, she thought

again about Heather. If for no other reason, she was glad she had written the article, she was happy to have gotten to know the younger girl.

Loud barking reached her ears long before her house came into view. Several of the neighborhood dogs, including Prince Albert, were prowling anxiously around the Wakefield garage, sniffing and barking with alarm.

"What on earth?"

Elizabeth opened the front door and followed the sound of her sister's voice into the kitchen. Jessica was on the telephone, her face flushed.

"What do you mean you have to keep it refrigerated?"

"But—"

"On the bottom of the jar? I never saw—"

"But how am I supposed to keep twelve cases—"

"So you mean it's rotting?"

There was a long pause as Jessica listened. Elizabeth looked at her twin and felt her anguish. Poor Jess! What a disaster!

Jessica's mouth was set in a determined line. "Well, then I'd like to return everything I haven't, so—"

"But I . . . No, but—"

Her chin was trembling as she said, "OK. I

understand." She hung up the phone in a daze and then turned to Elizabeth.

"Oh, Lizzie!" she wailed. "What am I going to do? I didn't know you had to keep the stuff cold! Whoever heard of putting shampoo in the refrigerator?" She covered her face with her hands. "It's not fair!"

"But, Jessica, they'll take it back, won't they?"

"No! They said since I let it spoil they can't be responsible for it. They said it's my own fault."

Elizabeth's heart sank. "And you gave a money-back—"

"I know!" Jessica burst into tears. "I have to buy every single bottle of rotting tofu back myself!" She lifted her tearstained face and repeated, "Oh, Lizzie! What am I going to do?"

Nine

"You look nice today, Liz."

Elizabeth looked up at Jeffrey. He was looking at her with a tender smile, and she blushed with pleasure.

"What did I do to deserve that?" she asked.

"Oh, nothing. Just being yourself."

"Well, that was easy enough!"

She shook her head, happy that the tension was gone. On Monday night she and Jeffrey had had a long talk. They had agreed that each was entitled to his or her own opinion and shouldn't feel pressured to change it. She felt relieved now that they had straightened it out, and her love for Jeffrey was stronger than ever. Now it was Thursday, and they were enjoying a peaceful truce on the subject of Aaron Dallas.

Of course Aaron was still angry about her article. He refused to speak to her, and didn't hesitate to tell anyone *how* angry he was,

Heather and Elizabeth avoided each other simply to keep the peace. But they smiled whenever they met, both feeling silly that they had to go through such a dumb farce.

"Ready for lunch?" Jeffrey continued, pulling a book from his locker.

She nodded. "And I'm starving, too."

"Then let's go." He offered her his arm, and laughing, she took it.

They walked outside so they could get to the outdoor eating area without going through the jammed cafeteria. It was a glorious, sunny day, typical for Sweet Valley. And the level of excitement about the big game that afternoon was high. Jeffrey was stopped several times by students who asked about the game and gave him their best wishes.

"Hey, good luck, Jeffrey," John Pfeifer called. "I'll be there!"

"Be sure to get an interview with the champs, then."

The sports editor for *The Oracle* laughed. "Why don't I just take your statement now? I'm sure you have a speech prepared already!"

Jeffrey grinned, and Elizabeth's heart filled with pride as she watched him.

"Well, anyway, good luck," John repeated.

"Yeah," added Mark Riley, a member of the track team. "Go for it."

"Everybody's so psyched up," Elizabeth marveled after the fifth person had wished Jeffrey luck. "It's the only thing people talk about. No offense, but who would have thought Sweet Valley High would go soccer crazy?"

He smiled proudly as they started walking again. "It's because we're going to win that trophy today, Liz. Everyone knows it," he said with a twinkle in his green eyes.

"And it'll be because of you," she said teasingly.

"Absolutely right!"

Suddenly the two found themselves on a collision course with Aaron Dallas and Heather Sanford, who had just walked outside from the cafeteria. The smiles faded quickly from their faces, and there was an awkward pause. Both couples stopped. Then Elizabeth saw Heather take Aaron's arm and urge him forward.

"Hi," Heather said with a friendly smile.

"Hi, Heather. Hi, Aaron."

There was a tense silence. Everyone waited for Aaron to say something. He stood rigidly closemouthed, looking over Elizabeth's shoulder, and she found herself getting angry with him and his childish obstinacy.

Jeffrey, never one to play games, stepped forward impatiently.

"Look, Aaron. Just forget it, OK? Liz did what she thought she had to do, so there's no point in staying mad about it, right?"

Aaron's handsome face remained impassive.

"Aaron?" Heather said softly. "Let's not let this get in the way of our friendships. Please?"

He turned to look at her and then glanced at Elizabeth coldly. "There's no friendship between her and me anyway, so don't worry."

"Aaron!" Jeffrey looked as though he'd been slapped in the face. "What are you talking about?"

"I don't consider your girlfriend a friend of mine."

Elizabeth's heart was pounding, and she knew her face was bright red. She also realized that Jeffrey, who was usually slow to get angry, was showing signs of losing his temper.

"Listen," Jeffrey said carefully. "It's over with, OK? The game's this afternoon, and you're going to play in it. So just forget about it, all right?"

Aaron refused to answer, and Jeffrey's voice rose angrily.

"Come on! You're really being stupid about this. Just grow up and forget it. It's no big deal!"

The two girls looked at each other, their eyes wide with alarm as they waited for Aaron's reply. Elizabeth prayed silently that the whole episode would blow over. But it was clear Aaron wasn't giving in. Maybe she should say something.

"Aaron, I was just reporting what I saw. I didn't mean it as a personal insult. I was covering practice, and that's what happened that day."

He looked steadily at Jeffrey. "I'm waiting for her to apologize."

"Apologize!" Elizabeth gasped. She couldn't believe what he was saying. A small crowd was gathering around them, and she felt her cheeks burn with embarrassment and indignation.

"You seem to think that everyone owes you an apology these days," Jeffrey responded hotly. "But maybe you're the one who should be apologizing, like to Brad, for one!"

"Oh, yeah? So now you're against me, too, right?"

"Jeez, Aaron! Grow up, will you? Stop acting like a spoiled brat."

Suddenly Aaron lost whatever control he had left, and before anyone realized what was happening, he threw himself at Jeffrey and punched him in the mouth.

"Jeffrey!" Elizabeth screamed.

The impact threw him backward into the crowd, and there was a moment of shocked silence. All eyes were on Aaron Dallas as he looked down at his best friend, an expression of utter disbelief and horror on his face.

Then he spun around and tore blindly across the lawn.

Tears streamed down Heather's face. She moved toward Jeffrey, her hand outstretched. "Oh, God! I'm—I'm—!" She turned and raced after Aaron.

Elizabeth helped Jeffrey to his feet. He rubbed his chin. His lower lip was beginning to swell up.

The two exchanged a look of sadness, and then they turned and saw the two figures disappearing around the corner of the building. Jeffrey closed his eyes and sighed.

"He's off the team," someone in the crowd said in an excited voice. "That's what the coach said, right? One more fight, and he's off the team."

"Then he'll miss the game today," someone added.

Jeffrey's eyes flew open, and he stared across the campus. "Aaron," he whispered. "What have you done?"

"Aaron! Aaron, please! Stop!" Heather sobbed, her breath coming in short, painful gasps.

He plunged on ahead of her, and she chased

him frantically, stumbling, until they reached the far end of the parking lot. He stopped beside a green station wagon and leaned against the hood, his shoulders heaving.

"Oh, Aaron," she whispered, putting her arms around him. They stood without speaking for a long time as tears rolled down Aaron's cheeks.

"I can't believe it!" he said, wiping away a tear with his fist. "I can't believe I hit Jeffrey! My best friend, and I hit him!"

Heather nodded mutely. She was afraid to speak, and afraid not to. She desperately hoped he would finally see how irrationally he had been behaving, but maybe he was too upset to think clearly. She didn't know what to do, but finally she decided to let him talk it out himself.

With a great effort of will, Aaron pulled himself together. He leaned back against the car and looked out into the distance. Heather gave silent thanks that she was there with him.

"You know," he began slowly, speaking as though in a dream, "my dad did that to me once. He says I'm the most important person in the world to him, but he hit me once. I couldn't believe it. And now I did it, too."

He sighed heavily and looked at Heather, his eyes full of pain. "I know how Jeffrey must feel right now."

She took his hand with a tender smile. "Maybe this is a good time to try doing something about it—you know, about how you get so mad."

"What do you mean?"

"Maybe you could talk to somebody who knows about these things. Don't you think you could use some help?"

He winced. "But I've got you, Heather. You understand."

"Oh, Aaron! I want to, but I don't! Don't you see? I can't help you all by myself." She felt a sob welling up in her throat and fought to keep it back. "I love you, Aaron. And I want to help you, but I think you need more than just me."

"Oh, come on, Heather!" he said, his voice rising again.

Her heart beating frantically, Heather shook her head. She stood straight and defiant. "Don't yell anymore, Aaron! You've got to stop!" He gritted his teeth, and she repeated, "You've got to stop!"

"Oh, Heather!" he cried, pounding his fist on the car roof. "What am I going to do?"

"Why not start with Mrs. Green? That's what guidance counselors are for, right?"

He made a sour face. "But what if my dad finds out? He'll kill me."

"No, he won't!" she said. "Your father needs

help, too. Don't you see that?'' They had never talked so openly before, and Heather was afraid, afraid that their relationship would come crashing down around her if she said everything. But she knew she had to say it.

"Aaron, your parents are getting divorced! That's real, and you can't change that.''

He looked at her silently, only his eyes betraying the anguish he was feeling.

"So you have to learn to accept it—live with it. Don't keep bottling all your emotions up inside. That's why you get so mad, I think.'' Her hands were shaking, and she looked anxiously into his face, hoping to see some sign that he understood what she was saying.

"Maybe you're right,'' he whispered hoarsely. "Maybe I have been trying to pretend it isn't happening,'' he admitted.

"Aaron, it's OK to admit you need help. No one ever said you had to deal with this kind of pain all by yourself!''

He looked into her eyes. "How can you be so nice to me?'' he wondered out loud. "If I were you I'd hate me for being such a jerk.''

"Oh, Aaron,'' she said tenderly. "I love you.''

They were silent for a moment, feeling the newer, deeper love they shared.

"Let's go see Mrs. Green, OK?''

He nodded wearily.

"But, first, why don't we find Jeffrey? Tell him you're going to work this out. And you can tell him you're sorry."

"He'll never forgive me for hitting him."

"Of course he will, Aaron!"

But he shook his head bitterly. "I've never forgiven my dad."

Within minutes of the fight the campus was buzzing with the news: Aaron Dallas had punched his best friend, Jeffrey French. And he would be kicked off the team. Sweet Valley High didn't stand a chance without him! The finals that afternoon would be a first-class disaster.

"Jessica!" Cara called, running breathlessly to catch up with her friend. "Did you hear what happened?"

Jessica narrowed her eyes. "Cara, believe me. Jeffrey would never hit anyone."

"No! It was the other way around. They were in a fight about Liz! And Aaron hit Jeffrey!"

The two girls walked together to the cafeteria. "Don't you think that's pretty amazing?" Cara prodded.

Jessica shrugged.

"Well, come on! Liz's article said Aaron would get kicked off the team if he got into another fight, right? So he can't play this afternoon."

"Who cares?" Jessica asked. She was too caught up in her own problems to care whether Aaron Dallas played in the soccer finals. "There are a lot worse things in the world, you know."

Cara stopped walking and stared at her friend. "Boy, what concern! What's the matter? Still stuck with that disgusting tofu?"

"Give me a break, will you? Don't rub it in."

"I thought that was the problem," Cara said teasingly. "That you can't rub it in. Or rinse it out."

Jessica spun around. "For your information, Cara, I've lost every single penny I made, plus I owe Liz a ton of money, plus I have a whole garage full of rotting tofu, plus my mom is ready to kill me if I don't get rid of it. Plus," she added, seething with indignation, "every single dog in Sweet Valley is snooping around the house, trying to figure out what the smell is. There, satisfied?"

She saw Cara trying to suppress a grin. "Don't laugh," she said, starting to walk away. "It's the most horrible and humiliating thing that's ever happened to me in my whole life."

Ten

Elizabeth set down two sodas and joined Jeffrey on the bench.

"How's your chin?" she asked quietly. She sensed that he was more upset than he let on.

He shrugged. "It's OK, I guess. Aaron throws a fantastic right hook," he added wryly.

"I'm surprised you can joke about it," Elizabeth began. But the look on his face cut her off.

"What else can I do?" He shook his head sadly. "My best friend just blew his top and slugged me. I don't know whether to cry or be angry or what! It's just unbelievable."

"Not so unbelievable, Jeffrey."

He sighed and looked into her eyes soberly. "Maybe not to you, and it shouldn't have been to me, I guess. I just didn't want to listen to you."

"Do you believe me now?" Elizabeth asked,

her voice gentle. There was no satisfaction in being proven right. It broke her heart to think that it took a punch in the jaw for Jeffrey to see what was really happening to Aaron.

"Oh, Liz," he said, exhaling slowly. He stared across the lawn. "I can see now that he's got a serious problem. And I guess I wasn't doing him much good by ignoring it."

Elizabeth didn't say anything. She stared into her soda, absently watching the bubbles rise to the surface. She let him continue.

"What a jerk I was. All those times I kept telling him he was right to get mad. I was so blind."

"Well, now you know, right?"

He shifted uncomfortably on the bench. "Yeah, but what can I do? I mean, I don't know if it's any of my business. I can't tell him what he should do!"

"Jeffrey, come on! Make it your business. Aaron's supposed to be your best friend."

He looked at her, his expression blank. "So what do I do?"

Elizabeth drew a deep breath, thinking hard. Even though she knew that Aaron had a serious problem, she hadn't really considered what it meant. "I don't know," she said honestly. "All you can do is be his friend. Talk to him, see whether he realizes it himself yet. I guess that would be a good first step."

"But, Liz! That doesn't sound like a very long-range solution, you know. No. He's got to really *do* something more than just admit he's got a problem, right?"

They looked at each other silently for a moment.

"Maybe he should see some kind of professional counselor or therapist," Elizabeth suggested finally, voicing what was on both of their minds.

Jeffrey didn't say anything, and the silence became heavy between them. If Aaron's problems were serious enough for him to need professional help, then maybe they were more serious than his friends thought.

But suddenly Jeffrey chuckled. "Hey, come on! It's not as if Aaron's psychotic! He's just got an emotional problem, and he should see a therapist. Big deal."

"Because of his parents' divorce," Elizabeth added.

"Right. So I know lots of kids who have gone to see therapists, and for less serious problems than divorce."

Elizabeth nodded, thinking back over all the times when she had had problems. There had been some times when she'd almost sought help herself. At least she had Jessica, her parents, Enid, Mr. Collins, and Jeffrey.

But some kids didn't feel that they had any-body. And thinking you were all alone was the worst feeling in the world, she knew.

"We should really try to get him to see someone," Jeffrey continued firmly. "He might try to punch me out again, but I'm going to tell him!"

His raised voice attracted some curious stares from nearby students. Elizabeth wondered if people thought Jeffrey was mad at Aaron. But who cared what they thought. She knew how loyal Jeffrey always was to his friends. He wouldn't let Aaron down, no matter what.

She glanced at Jeffrey again, feeling a warm glow of love and admiration. "Maybe he'll listen to you," she said hopefully. "If he's half as smart as he used to be, he'll know you want the best for him."

He laughed. "Even if it kills him!" But he was instantly serious again. "There's one prob-lem, though." He broke off and looked at the crowds milling around.

"Well?"

"There's no way Coach Horner won't have heard about Aaron punching me, and he'll kick Aaron off the team!"

"I know, but—" Elizabeth was puzzled. "I mean, other than missing the game today, will it really matter that much?"

"Matter? Liz, you don't have any idea how important playing soccer is to him. I think it helps him to know there's one thing in his life that he's good at, that's always there for him." Jeffrey shook his head sadly. "Getting kicked off the team would kill him."

"But, Jeffrey, don't you think there's a chance that that'll just show him how much he has to work out this problem? Won't it make it that much more obvious?"

He shrugged. "I don't know. Maybe, but it'll still be awful for him. I'm sure of that."

And for the team, Elizabeth added silently. But she realized that Jeffrey was probably right, and it broke her heart to think about the added anguish Aaron would go through.

"Maybe the coach won't find out right away," she said hopefully. "Then at least Aaron could play in the game this afternoon."

He shook his head. "Maybe, but I doubt it."

For a moment they ate in silence, thinking over everything that had just happened. Suddenly Jeffrey stood up, his lunch still barely eaten. "I've got to find him and straighten this whole thing out."

Elizabeth stood up, too. "Do you think I should come?"

"Are you kidding?" He smiled at her. "Of course. I want you to be there. Come on."

Aaron took Heather's hand. "OK. Let's go."

She smiled up at him, that smile that meant so much to him. He realized if it weren't for her and soccer, he would probably have fallen apart a long time ago.

"Aaron?"

With a start, he came back to the present. He gave her a guilty smile. "I was just thinking about how much I love you."

"Aaron—"

"No—" He put one finger on her lips. "Let's just go find Jeffrey, OK?"

She smiled, obviously relieved. "Right."

As they made their way back across campus, Aaron thought about all of his recent wild rages. Had he been wrong every time? he wondered, a flush of shame heating his face. *Probably,* he thought. But even if he hadn't been wrong, he never should have gotten into fights about mixed-up line calls or getting knocked down.

Somehow admitting his mistakes made him feel relieved. He knew that he wasn't really angry at all those people and incidents. It was the other thing, the divorce. He made himself say the word silently. *Divorce.*

It was time he admitted it. He was torn up about his parents' splitting up. Living with just his dad was so different from living with both his parents. He didn't think he could ever get used to the silent dinners in front of the TV or the look of pain in his father's eyes.

Heather nudged him, and he looked up. Jeffrey and Elizabeth were coming toward them. He drew a deep breath and stopped in front of his friend.

"Jeffrey, I—"

"Hey, Aaron, it's—"

The two boys spoke at once, then there was an embarrassed pause. Aaron knew everyone was waiting for him to say something, and he was keenly aware of Elizabeth's eyes on him. Involuntarily he clenched his jaw, trying to put her out of his mind.

"Look, Jeffrey, I'm really sorry," he began again. He held up his hand, asking them to let him speak. "There's really no excuse at all for what I did, and I'm really, really sorry."

"Hey, no problem, Aaron. I understand." Jeffrey put his hand out, and Aaron took it gratefully. "So we can forget all that stuff and get back to being friends, right?"

Aaron froze. He knew exactly what Jeffrey meant: forget about the article Liz wrote. But every time he thought about it, he felt his anger starting all over again. He just couldn't get over it. Elizabeth Wakefield had humiliated him in front of the entire school.

But didn't you humiliate yourself? a nagging little voice inside him prodded. He shook his head and turned to Jeffrey again.

"I—I guess so."

Heather and Elizabeth each breathed a sigh of relief. "I'm really glad, Aaron," Elizabeth said, giving him a warm smile.

He met her eyes briefly and then looked away. But when he met Jeffrey's look, he knew he had to say something. He had to say something if he expected Jeffrey to continue to be his friend.

"Me, too," he said gruffly.

An awkward silence descended on the group.

"Are you still mad at Liz?" Jeffrey asked with a bluntness that made Aaron wince. "Are you?"

"Well, what if I am?" he snapped back. Instantly, he regretted his words.

Jeffrey took a deep breath. "Maybe it's time you took a good look at yourself, Aaron. You've got to do something about that temper of yours. Maybe you should see some kind of professional—"

"Like a shrink? Is that what you think? That I'm crazy or something?"

"Aaron, come on," Heather whispered, taking his arm. "We decided that he should talk to Mrs. Green first," she said frankly to Jeffrey and Elizabeth. "It's a good place to start."

Aaron felt his shoulders sag. He forced himself to look Jeffrey in the eye.

"That's right," he said, trying to keep his voice steady. "I do want some help."

"Aaron?" It was Elizabeth. "Aaron, I'm sorry. I can understand how you might have thought the article was unfair." She smiled. "Can't we still be friends?"

All eyes were on him. *Say yes*, he told himself.

The tension mounted as he struggled with himself. But Elizabeth's smile did not waver.

"Sure," he said, letting his breath out slowly.

There was a collective sigh of relief. Aaron felt as though a weight had suddenly been lifted from his shoulders.

"I'm sorry, too," he said, returning her smile at last.

Heather squeezed his hand, and he smiled tenderly at her.

"Hey, why are we just standing around?" Jeffrey asked, now that the atmosphere finally relaxed. "Let's go sit under that tree."

Everyone agreed, and in a moment they were seated in the shade. They shared shy smiles with one another. There was a feeling that they had all gone through something important together.

"So when are you going to see Mrs. Green?" Jeffrey asked, his voice casual.

Aaron glanced at his watch. It seemed impossible to believe that from the time he had hit Jeffrey until then, only thirty minutes had passed. It felt more like a lifetime. He made a quick, but serious, decision.

"Right now."

The others exchanged meaningful looks. Aaron noticed it, but he shook his head. "Listen, if I get kicked off the team, it's nobody's fault but mine."

"You could wait till tomorrow, though, couldn't you?" Jeffrey suggested, raising his eyebrows.

He shook his head. "No. Hey, look. There's no way the coach won't hear about this, so I'm off the team anyway. I just want to get it over with."

"But maybe he won't find out!" Jeffrey persisted. "Nobody wants to see you off the team. No one's going to tell him."

Aaron's heart leaped at the thought of staying on the team, of playing in the finals. Being in that game would be great!

But he knew it wasn't fair. He couldn't quite put it into words, but if Jeffrey was a good enough friend to forget the fight, then Aaron had to go see Mrs. Green—as soon as possible.

"Maybe not," he said. "But I'm going now. I'm going to tell Mrs. Green. And if I get kicked off the team, it's because I deserve it." He gave Heather a quick kiss, then walked off toward the school.

Eleven

Elizabeth gazed at Aaron's retreating figure, her mind whirling with conflicting ideas and emotions. After all the moments of anger and impatience with Aaron, she now felt a surge of respect and friendship.

A sound behind her made her turn. Heather was wiping away a tear, and she sniffed. But she was smiling in spite of it.

"What is it, Heather?" asked Elizabeth.

The girl sighed. "I'm really glad he's going, that's all. But I know how much it'll hurt him to get taken off the team. Mrs. Green will have to tell the coach, won't she?"

"No, she can't." Jeffrey spoke up suddenly. "Guidance counselors have to keep things confidential."

"Really? I mean, she really won't tell?" Heather's eyes were still bright with tears, and she looked off toward the direction in which Aaron had gone.

Elizabeth reached for Heather's hand. "No, but I think Aaron might. I think he'll want the coach to know."

"But then he'll be off the team! Oh, Liz! It'll be so hard for him."

"We'll just have to wait and see what happens," said Elizabeth softly.

Heather squared her shoulders and nodded. "You're right. I'm just being a softy."

"It's just because you care about him so much, that's all."

Heather smiled gratefully at her.

"Listen, don't worry about it, OK?" Elizabeth glanced at her watch and gasped. "I don't know about you, but I'm about to be late for class."

Jeffrey stood up. "How about we try to meet Aaron at Mrs. Green's office at the end of this period—if he's still there, that is." He looked down at the two girls. "Because if he's off the team, he's going to need some real friends."

"How would you feel about that, Aaron? Being taken off the soccer team?"

He looked across the desk at Mrs. Green, trying to find the right words. He'd been trying to explain himself for the past twenty minutes. "I don't know," he finally answered lamely. *Boy, does that sound dumb!* he said, scolding himself.

"Would you be glad? Relieved?"

"No!" He paused, still grappling with his emotions. "I'd hate it, Mrs. Green. I really would."

"Then why do you want me to tell Coach Horner?"

Aaron shook his head silently.

The guidance counselor drew a deep breath and noticed him glance at the clock. "Do you have anything important this period, any tests?"

"No."

"Then don't worry about cutting class. I'll sign a pass for you."

He nodded again. It was so easy to let this warm, friendly woman tell him what to do. Finally, somebody was going to help him get things straightened out.

"Now I'd like to talk about your options, Aaron. I agree that you would benefit greatly from talking to somebody. But it doesn't have to be a psychiatrist or a psychologist or any other kind of 'ist.'" She smiled sympathetically. "So don't worry. You could even just talk to plain old me if you want to."

"But, Mrs. Green, don't I—I mean . . ." He faltered, blushing hotly. "Don't you think I have some kind of emotional problem?"

With a peal of laughter, Mrs. Green shook her head. "Oh, Aaron! Don't look so serious!" She paused, then spoke gently again. "I'm sorry. I'm not laughing at you. But to answer your question, yes, you do, but it's not the end of the world! I want you to understand that."

He swallowed with difficulty. Maybe things weren't so bad after all, he thought, hope growing. "OK," he said, meeting her level gaze. "So what do I do?"

"Well, first I'd like to call your father."

Aaron froze. "Why?" he managed to whisper.

"Because I think he should be part of this. Aaron, listen. I'm not 'telling' on you."

He looked away. Had he made a huge mistake coming there? he wondered in anguish. No, another voice told him. He had to trust Mrs. Green. Taking a deep breath, he met her gaze again.

"Aaron, from what you've told me your father is involved in what you're going through, and if you try to work it out together, I think you'll solve this a lot faster."

"OK," he agreed slowly, his heart pounding. "I guess that makes sense."

Mrs. Green paused a moment. Then she said, "Have you ever said anything to your dad about this divorce? Does he know how you feel?"

"No."

For a moment it seemed as if she was going to say something about that, but she let it pass. "What's your father's number at work?"

He gave it to her and then sank back into his chair, letting her voice drift over him. She spoke at length with his father, but he hardly heard her words. All he knew was that now he had to talk to his dad and his dad would have to talk to him. It was frightening, in a way. Their silence was easy. Breaking it would be hard.

The tone of Mrs. Green's voice changed, and he focused his attention on her again. She was smiling, and she bade his father a cheerful goodbye.

"Well, I think that's a good start," she said, giving him a friendly smile.

"He wasn't mad?"

"Of course not, Aaron. He wants to help you—and himself."

Suddenly Aaron's throat tightened, and he was terrified that he might start to cry in front of Mrs. Green. She looked casually out the window.

Once he had controlled himself, he looked up again, thanking her silently for giving him a few moments to recover.

"Now, are you ready to talk to your coach?"

He hesitated a brief second and then nodded. "Yeah. I guess so."

Elizabeth and Heather both arrived outside the guidance office at the same moment. Elizabeth gave her friend an encouraging smile.

"Is he still in there, do you think?"

Heather shook her head. "I don't know. I—I hate to knock."

"Well, don't worry. We can ask—"

At that moment the door of Mrs. Green's office opened, and Coach Horner walked out, his face expressionless. Heather took a step forward. But she didn't speak.

Elizabeth was dying to know what had gone on inside the office, but she didn't dare ask. She bit her lip.

The coach glanced at the two girls and turned down the hallway. In a moment he was out of sight around a corner.

"Do you think? . . ." Heather's eyes were wide.

Elizabeth shook her head silently.

"What's going on?" Jeffrey asked, coming upon them suddenly. He was slightly out of breath, and he looked back over his shoulder. "I just passed the coach. Was he in there?"

Both girls nodded.

"Is Aaron—"

Heather nodded quickly. "I think so."

The three stood awkwardly in front of the door, waiting for their friend. Their nervousness increased as the minutes ticked by.

"I should really get to class," Jeffrey said to no one in particular.

Elizabeth nodded. "Me, too."

But nobody moved.

"Well, what's happening in there? He's been talking to her since before last period!"

Elizabeth nodded again. And still no one left.

"I wonder if—"

The door opened, and Aaron stood framed in the opening, Mrs. Green behind him.

"Aaron!"

"What happened?"

"What did the coach say?"

Aaron looked questioningly at Mrs. Green. She gave him a smile and a nod and then stepped back into her office, closing the door.

"Let's go outside a minute," Aaron said, his voice quivering with suppressed excitement.

Elizabeth sensed that Aaron had good news, better than they had hoped for. But she and the others kept silent until Aaron was ready to tell them what it was.

Finally he stopped and turned to them with

an air of triumph. "I'm still on the team," he announced.

"You are? That's fantastic!" Jeffrey cried, clapping his friend on the back.

"But how?"

It was Heather who spoke, her voice low and insistent. She stared at Aaron intently, searching his face for clues to what had happened in the office.

Aaron turned to her, his expression serious again. "Mrs. Green and I decided we should tell the coach," he explained. "But when he got there—well, I was so blown away, I didn't know what to say!"

"What do you mean?"

"Well, Mrs. Green told him about me punching Jeffrey," he continued, smiling apologetically at his friend. "And he really started to tear into me. But she said that what would really help me would be my staying on the team."

Jeffrey let out a low whistle. "She said that? And he agreed?"

"Yeah. Because—well, she knew how much it means to me and—" Aaron broke off, obviously struggling with his emotions. "And I swore I'd make them both proud of me. Coach won't be sorry he gave me another chance."

"All right!" Jeffrey crowed, his eyes dancing with happiness and excitement. "That is so great! I can't believe it!"

Heather put her arms around Aaron and hugged him. Then she pulled away. "But, Aaron, what about—you know."

Elizabeth looked at Heather with new respect. Instead of getting excited about Aaron's staying on the team, Heather wanted to know about the real problem.

He nodded. "First we called my dad, and he agreed to go to counseling with me." He rummaged in his pocket and pulled out a slip of paper. "This is a guy who does family counseling. Mrs. Green says he works a lot with kids whose parents are splitting up."

"And you think it'll work?" Heather asked.

Aaron put his arm around her shoulders. "I don't know, Heather. But I'm going to give it a try. And you know?" he added, a soft smile lighting up his face. "I already feel a lot better, like nothing could ever make me get so mad again." He stopped suddenly, blushing, and looked away.

Without putting it into words, Elizabeth realized how hard it must be for Aaron to talk so openly to them about himself, and she felt a pang of remorse and sympathy. She and Jeffrey shouldn't be there. It was for Aaron and Heather to discuss. She looked at Jeffrey and caught his eye.

"We'd better get to class," she said, breaking the uneasy silence. "Better late than never."

He understood. "Hey, see you later, you guys," he said, waving to Aaron and Heather. "See you at the game!"

Then he and Elizabeth walked away.

"He's going to make it," Jeffrey said once they were out of earshot. "He's going to be OK."

Elizabeth glanced back over her shoulder. Aaron and Heather were standing together with their arms around each other, not speaking.

"You're right," she said, looking up into his eyes and loving what she saw there. "With friends like you and Heather, he can't lose."

Twelve

"Liz! Hurry up!"

Elizabeth slammed her locker shut and dashed off after Enid.

"I'm coming, I'm coming!" She caught up to her friend. "But what's the huge rush? The game doesn't start until three!"

Enid fixed her with a stern eye as they hurried across the lawn. "Maybe not, but even if you forgot your obligation as an unofficial cheerleader, I haven't. You've got to give that boy of yours some encouragement."

"Oh, Enid, be serious!"

As they approached the soccer field, they joined some other girls who were hurrying to the game, DeeDee Gordon, Penny Ayala, Susan Stewart, Sally Larson, and Caroline Pearce. Soon they had a small group of friends with them, and there was much excited speculation and discussion about the game as they found seats on the sidelines.

"But with Aaron off the team, it's going to be tough," Susan commented. "He made all the difference. I just don't see how we can make it without him."

"But he's not off the team," Elizabeth said, turning to Susan. "He's in the game today."

"But how? Didn't the coach hear about Aaron fighting with Jeffrey?"

Elizabeth cocked her head to one side. "Yes, but it wasn't exactly a fight, you know."

"Well, whatever," Enid cut in excitedly. "Why didn't he get kicked off?"

Elizabeth paused, choosing her words carefully. "Coach Horner is giving him another chance, that's all."

Looking at the bewildered, wondering faces around her, Elizabeth knew that her explanation wasn't entirely satisfactory. But she also knew that she couldn't go into the details about Aaron's talk with Mrs. Green to her friends. It wasn't her business to divulge that information.

"Liz! What do you know?" Enid looked at her accusingly. "Come on. I order you to confess!"

"Aaron just agreed that he'd do whatever he could to control his temper," Elizabeth finished. That was all the explanation she was willing to give.

"So no more temper tantrums, huh?"

"I guess not."

Penny Ayala chuckled. "Then does that mean we don't get to hear Heather taming the savage beast with her baby talk?" She shook her head with mock sadness. "That would really be a shame."

"Oh, no!" DeeDee said, laughing, too. "You'll just have to do your imitation of her, Liz. It was the funniest thing I ever heard. That's the only compensation." She turned to Susan and said, "You weren't at the Tofu-Glo party when Liz did her impersonation of Aaron's girlfriend. It was hysterical."

Susan laughed. "Oh, no fair. You have to do it, so I can hear it, too."

There was a general cry of "Yes, come on Liz," and "Do your imitation of Heather," from the girls sitting around her on the bleachers.

She shook her head and smiled. "No, not right now." *Never again*, she added silently. Since she had gotten to know Heather, she had learned to like and respect the girl. Now she couldn't imagine making fun of her and was ashamed that she ever had.

"Oh, come on, Liz. It was perfect!"

"No, I really don't want to," she insisted.

Actually," came Heather's voice, "my sister does the best imitation of me." Everyone had been so busy talking that no one had seen Heather walking up the steps of the bleachers.

Everyone looked at her in embarrassed surprise. Elizabeth blushed furiously, hating herself.

But Heather seemed unperturbed. She smiled at the small group and sat down beside them, smoothing her skirt with a characteristic gesture.

"What did E.W. say that made A.D. so mad?" she asked, looking at the assembled girls with a grave face. "And they say J.F. avenged his ladylove with stern words. A bout of ferocious and furious fisticuffs followed."

Her eyes wide with amusement, Elizabeth burst into laughter. Heather was making up a fictitious item from "Eyes and Ears," the gossip column Elizabeth wrote every week for *The Oracle*. And not only that, but the girl was mimicking Elizabeth's own voice and mannerisms perfectly.

As the others caught on, they started giggling, too. But Heather didn't stop her imaginative chattering. "I hear a certain serious student with the initials P.A. cut English class today," she said glibly, casting a quick, impish look at Penny Ayala.

This was greeted with howls of laughter, and Heather continued. "Also, this just in:

E.R. was seen recently buying seven pints of pistachio ice cream at the Qwik Stop MiniMart. Do her friends know about this shocking addiction?"

"It's not true!" Enid giggled hysterically. "I've been framed!"

Elizabeth shook her head solemnly. "Oh, Enid. I never knew! How horrible!"

"And finally," Heather concluded, as the soccer players began to run onto the field, "who will win this week's crucial game? Our own brave boys, or Big Mesa?"

A chorus of boos and hisses mingled with giggles greeted that question. At the end of Heather's recital, the girls burst into applause, and Heather finally collapsed into her own fit of laughter.

"Heather, that was so embarrassing," Elizabeth teased. "I don't know if I can ever forgive you."

"Oh, you will." The girl sighed and wiped away a tear. "You will!"

Just then the whistle blew to begin the game, and the girls exchanged a smile of friendship.

"Good luck to you, for Aaron," Elizabeth said softly.

"Same to you, for Jeffrey."

Then they turned their attention to the game.

The first half of the game flew by, the competition fierce but evenly matched. There was one tense moment, though, when Aaron was tripped and fell flat on the ground. Elizabeth and Heather both held their breath, waiting for the outburst they were afraid might come. But Aaron just got up, brushed himself off, and raced back into the action. He and Jeffrey shook hands quickly on the field, grinning.

In the end Sweet Valley High emerged victorious, thanks largely to Aaron's skillful leadership. As he jumped into the air after his final goal, his teammates hugged him and clapped him on the back. They were ahead four to three and there were only seconds left to play.

Big Mesa made a brave show of playing out the final seconds, but when the whistle blew, the spectators ran screaming onto the field, surrounding the Sweet Valley team. Elizabeth and Heather tried to reach Jeffrey and Aaron, but it was almost impossible to get close.

"What do we do now?" Heather asked as she was being jostled by the excited crowd.

Elizabeth shrugged. "Yell!"

Through the tumult it was agreed that Heather, Aaron, and Jeffrey would go home with Elizabeth for a victory celebration. As soon as the boys were changed and ready, the four headed to the Wakefield house.

*   *   *

146

Jessica was practically in tears. That morning she had had to make a frantic, depressing phone call to the sanitation company to arrange for them to pick up the Tofu products.

"Fifty dollars to take it away?" she had wailed to the gruff-voiced sanitation worker. "Don't you pick it up for free?"

"Lady, what do you think we are? A philanthropic organization or something? Fifty bucks, that's as low as I go."

"OK," she had gasped weakly, clutching the phone desperately. "But can you come today?"

"Well—sure, for another ten bucks. But not before five o'clock."

She closed her eyes, swallowing the indignant protest that rose automatically to her lips. He might charge more if she was rude, she worried. Who could tell what he'd be capable of doing?

Reluctantly, Jessica had made the arrangements and given her address. Now the fluorescent orange truck from Dirty Don's Disposal was in the driveway, belching out diesel fumes into the already Tofu-scented air. The neighborhood dogs circled suspiciously, snarling in alarm, their heads low.

Jessica was miserable. She had had to race home immediately after the game instead of going out with some of the soccer players to celebrate, as the other cheerleaders were doing. She had a splitting headache, and she felt utterly defeated and alone.

Hiding behind a curtain, Jessica peeked out the window. She couldn't bear to go out and witness her shameful—and malodorous—defeat. Box after box of Tofu-Glo sailed through the air from the depths of the garage into the waiting jaws of the garbage truck.

Dirty Don—she assumed that was who it was—wiped his hands on his filthy green pants and started walking to the front door. Beating a hasty retreat from the window, Jessica glanced in agony at the check in her hand, signed that morning by Alice Wakefield. Jessica had received stern instructions to remove the Tofu-Glo at once and to reimburse her parents for the cost.

With a sinking heart, Jessica opened the door.

"I'm done," the man said abruptly. "That's sixty-five bucks."

"You said sixty on the phone," Jessica protested weakly.

He sniffed loudly and shifted a stubby cigar to the other side of his mouth. "You didn't mention on the phone that the stuff stinks. Sixty-five bucks."

"OK, OK. How do I make out the check?"

"No checks."

Jessica's heart stopped, and she stared in utter horror at Dirty Don. Then her self-control gave way, and she dissolved into tears "But I—don't—have any—money!" she cried, holding out the check.

He shook his head, made a sour face, scratched his chin, and looked over his shoulder. "OK, OK. Quit bawling. Just write 'Dirty Don' and let me get that junk out of here, all right?"

Her fingers shaking, Jessica filled out the check and handed it over. Still struggling with her sobs, she closed the door on Dirty Don and the Tofu-Glo, then leaned back against the door, trying to compose herself.

With a furious grinding of gears and a loud gasp from the air brakes, the garbage truck pulled out of the driveway and rumbled down the street.

"I can't believe it," Jessica said, brushing away the last of her tears. "And Lila will never let me forget this one."

The door opened behind her suddenly, and she nearly fell backward into Jeffrey French's arms.

"Whoa!" Laughing, he helped her stand up straight. "I've heard of dropping in to see someone, but dropping out?"

"Hi, Jess," Elizabeth said. Beside her were Heather Sanford and Aaron Dallas. Both boys had their gym bags over their shoulders.

149

Jessica returned Heather's and Aaron's hellos halfheartedly.

"Wasn't that a great game?" Jeffrey said, grinning at her. "It was one of the best games this year."

Jessica shrugged and stepped back into the house. "Great," was all she said.

Elizabeth cast her a suspicious glance and turned to Jeffrey. "Hey, why don't you guys go into the kitchen and get something to eat? I'll be right in."

"What's wrong, Jess?" she asked the moment the others had disappeared down the hallway.

Jessica felt her tears start welling up again as she thought of the way she had been forced to spend the afternoon. "I had to pay this gross, dirty sanitation man sixty-five dollars to take the stupid Tofu-Glo to the dump."

"Oh, Jess! No!"

"Yes!" she exclaimed, her voice quivering with indignation. "Liz, it's so unfair!"

Her sister nodded sympathetically. "I'm really sorry it turned out this way. You were a really great saleswoman."

Jessica brightened momentarily. "I was, wasn't I?"

"Maybe you'll find something else you can sell."

"Something that doesn't rot, you mean? Like encyclopedias? Forget it!"

The phone rang, and Elizabeth ran across the hall to her father's study to answer it. Jessica slumped into a chair in the living room, her gloom returning.

"How am I ever going to pay Liz back?" she muttered to herself. "And Mom and Dad?" she moaned. "Now I'm more broke than ever, and I'll never be out of debt. I'll never be able to buy another thing or do anything fun, ever."

The sound of her twin's voice washed over her from the study, but she was too depressed to try to listen.

"Jess? It's for you."

"I don't want to talk to anybody. I'm going into seclusion for the rest of my life."

Elizabeth appeared in the doorway, a mysterious grin on her face. "It's Dad. I think you'd better talk to him."

Rolling her eyes, Jessica complained, "Why can't you talk to him?"

"Jess! Come on. He wants to talk to you."

"Oh, all right!" she said, heaving herself out of her chair. She stomped across to the study and lifted the receiver. "Hi, Daddy."

"Hi, Jess. Liz just told me you had the Tofu-Glo carted away. How much did it cost?"

"Oh, Dad! Did you have to call just to remind me to pay you back? I will, I swear!"

There was a pause before her father answered her. "No, honey," he said softly. "That's not it."

She gulped. "Then why did you?"

She heard her father clear his throat. "Well, you know I wasn't very satisfied with this Tofu-Glo company, even before all this happened. So I did some checking."

"Yeah?" Jessica fiddled idly with the desk blotter, wishing he would get to the point so she could go wallow in her misery. "So what happened?"

"It seems somebody had brought a suit against Tofu-Glo, someone who had a similar experience. Anyway, to make a long story short, the company lost the suit, and all Tofu-Glo girls are to be reimbursed for the money they sent to the company."

Jessica's heart leaped.

"And damages."

"Dad!" she shrieked. "You're kidding!"

He chuckled. "Now, it's only three hundred dollars in your case—"

"So I can pay back Liz? And you and Mom?"

"And you might even have a little left over."

Jessica's mind was spinning so fast she could hardly think. She had made money on Tofu-Glo after all! How lucky could one person be?

"Jess?"

"I'm here, Dad. I just can't believe it!"

"Well, OK, honey. But listen," he added

his voice solemn. "Just because you came out on your feet doesn't mean disasters always end up so well."

"I know, Dad. I know—"

"So let's not have any more get-rich-quick schemes. All right, Jess?"

She laughed. "No way, Dad! I'm never trying that again!"

Elizabeth glanced up, smiling, as Jessica strode into the kitchen to join their victory celebration.

"I am never in my life going to bother with another dumb money-making scheme," her twin declared, throwing herself into a chair. "I'm just going to be happy with what I have, that's all."

Elizabeth raised her eyebrows and gave her sister a skeptical glance. She didn't want to say so in front of her friends, but that was hard to believe. It seemed to be one of Jessica's habits to go tearing of on one wild goose chase after another, and Elizabeth didn't think the memory of Tofu-Glo would stop Jessica for long.

"Well, anyway, now you have more time for other things," she said optimistically. "Like your tennis and cheerleading and stuff."

Jessica's hand flew to her mouth. "Speaking of cheerleading! Guess what Robin Wilson told me today! Remember how Julie Porter's sister dropped out of school last year?"

"Yeah." Elizabeth saw Jeffrey give her a puzzled look—he hadn't lived there when Johanna Porter still had gone to Sweet Valley High. He probably didn't even know Julie had an older sister.

"Well, she's coming back! Can you believe it?" Jessica reached for an apple and bit into it. "I mean, honestly! The girl drops out because she fails almost every single class, and she's coming back? Give me a break."

"Maybe she had a lot of problems or something," Heather suggested. "And she wants to try again."

"No way. She was just too dumb. Everyone knew about it. It was pretty embarrassing."

Elizabeth looked down at the table, feeling slightly embarrassed for her twin. How could Jessica be so insensitive? And poor Johanna! But without a doubt, the girl would be hearing a lot worse when she returned to Sweet Valley High!

Will Johanna be able to succeed when she returns to school? Find out in Sweet Valley High #36, LAST CHANCE, available in May 1987.

Next month, the Wakefield twins travel to the country for a little SPRING FEVER, the latest Sweet Valley High Super Edition.